AFTER CLASS

ATHINA FERNWOOD

For the dreamers and adventurers,
who believe in the impossible.
And for those who find love and hope,
even in the most unexpected places.
This journey is for you.

Athina Fernwood

CHAPTER ONE

I t had been four days, and I was done crying over him. Four days of lying in bed, barely getting up to feed the cat, let alone cook food and shower. Four days of staring at the far wall where I had stupidly hung the one framed photograph we had together, the picture he had not really wanted to take because he hated pictures and he hated PDA. What had resulted was an awkward "couple-y" photo where I was smiling too wide to make up for the fact that he was not smiling at all, with his arm around my shoulders squishing me half-heartedly to his side.

When I actually thought about it, the last two years had been complete bullshit. Wasted. Why hadn't I left him six months in? Why hadn't I left him when I first even *suspected* he was sleeping around?

But nope. I had been so determined to make it work *"All good relationships take sacrifice, dear," as my mother used to say* that I had ignored every huge red flag. My own angry internal voice echoed the cruel last words Ethan Carter had said to me between drags on a cigarette in the Petco parking lot, as I stood there with tears streaming down my face holding a bag of cat food.

"You're just *weak*, Cass! God, you let me walk all over you. Of course I had to see how far I could push it! You've known about Sophia for weeks, come on, don't act surprised."

Weak. It brought on a fresh stream of tears. I guess I wasn't done crying.

"Yes you are!" Maya yelled from the other room. Beautiful, crazy, party-girl Maya Thompson. She had been my saving grace over the past few days. Coming over in the evenings to make sure I was eating something other than chicken-flavored ramen noodles. I felt awful, knowing she was worried about me. I felt awful in general.

Maya was the master of handling breakups. I had seen her go through three, and that girl was the quintessential "movie-style breakup" girl. She would get herself a big glass of wine, chug it on her way to the club, and vomit everything up at the end of the night as if she was literally purging out her ex. When I had seen her cry, it was angry tears. She would sit there and say, "He'll realize what he's missing. He'll fucking regret it. Watch him come crawling back in a month, Cass, just watch!"

I really, *really* wished I could do that. I wished I could see my own value. How sad is that? God.

"Come on girl, up, get out of that bed before you atrophy to it."

I opened my swollen eyes at Maya, who stood with her arms crossed over me. She had let herself in, as usual, so I hadn't actually seen her yet since she had been so preoccupied cleaning up my disastrous kitchen. Her long black hair was in a high ponytail, she had false lashes on, and was wearing a short off-the-shoulder red dress.

I sniffled. I had been wearing the same 5-year-old Victoria's Secret leggings and Ethan's old t-shirt for days. "What are you all dressed up for?"

"Because we're going *out*," she said, flinging back my blankets and then going to my closet, rifling through the hangers. "You've been in this apartment way too long. This isn't *healthy*, Cass. Why are you even sad? You know that guy was such an asshole. He was *always* an asshole. Two years and he wouldn't even meet your parents? Come *on*."

I sat up, realizing I really needed a shower. I also really needed to clean my room: there were five half-empty mugs of tea on my bedside table alone. I shuffled to the bathroom and turned the water on as hot as it would go. Just below scalding, *perfect*. When I caught a glimpse of myself in the mirror, I was honestly a little horrified. There were dark bags under my eyes, I looked like I had lost 5 pounds, and my brown hair was a complete rat's nest.

"Get it together, Cassandra," I said, frowning at my sad mirror-self. "Maya is right. Just get the hell over him already."

Body wash and hot water really do wonders. By the time I had blow-dried and straightened my hair, Maya had already chosen my outfit for the night: a little black dress with a strappy, harness-inspired cutout around the neck and above the very low-cut neckline. I had been so excited when I got that dress and Ethan had hated it. He had said it made me look slutty. So it had gone into the back of my closet, unworn. It actually still had the tags on it.

It still looked as good as when I had first tried it on. It made me feel like I could be one of those kinky porn girls, except my ass was too flat and my tits were too small. I made a mental note to buy a new push-up bra ASAP. Ethan had never liked those on me either.

Go figure, the girl he had left me for was a queen of short skirts and big cleavage.

We took an Uber downtown, Maya sneaking us vodka shots in an innocent-looking water bottle.

"Where are we even going?" I said. "You know my classes start tomorrow right? I really can't get too turned up." She looked at me incredulously. "*Really*, Maya, I can't."

"Okay, okay," she said, pouting a little. "We're going to Bailey's!"

"Oh god, *Bailey's*? Maya that's such a frat boy bar-"

"Yeah, exactly. Dozens of horny frat boys who are all gonna want a piece of hot Cass ass. *Trust me.* A little flirting, maybe making out with a stranger you'll never see again? It's good for your self-esteem."

I was pretty sure there had been studies published saying the exact opposite, but whatever. We were already there and I was three shots deep thanks to Maya's vodka. The Uber dropped us off right in front, where there was luckily no line. The bar was packed nonetheless, mostly college kids getting in their last night out before classes started up again. Maya and I wormed our way up to the bar where she ordered for us, and then put a bright blue drink in a plastic cup into my hand.

"Adios!" she said cheerily, and downed half of hers before dragging me out amongst the crowd.

The Chainsmokers was blasting over the sound system, a song that had been good the first time I heard it until I couldn't turn on the radio without it playing on every other station. I followed Maya around as she saw people she knew and went up to say hi, sipping my drinking and smiling and nodding appropriately. I never knew what to do with myself in bars. Clubs were easier, since I could just dance and pretend I was tripping out if I wanted someone to leave me alone. Luckily for me, Maya took most of the attention so I was spared having to get too involved talking with strangers. The drink was also taking a much more rapid affect than I had expected. Suddenly everything was feeling great.

Just great.

Of course Maya managed to latch on to some thickly-muscled hunk and disappeared onto the dance floor with him. "I'll be *right* back," she slurred. "*Right* back, okay Casszy, just stay right there."

I leaned against the bar where she had left me, setting down my empty cup. My head was feeling light, and everything felt a little numb. Definitely drunk. Crap. A guy offered to buy me a drink, but he honestly looked just a little too much like Ethan. I lied and told him I was waiting for my boyfriend to get back, motioning in the general direction of the bathroom.

And that's when I saw him.

He was sitting at one of the few tall round tables in the place, chin resting on his fist. He looked like someone had picked him up out of a library and plopped him into a bar. He had tousled dark blonde hair, with a slim build and cheekbones sharp enough to cut a girl. Damn. Thin silver glasses sat on his nose, and he was . . . actually reading a book?

In a bar?

The liquor was giving me courage, and with a deep breath I sidled over.

"Hi," I said, trying to seem casual and confident. He glanced up at me in surprise, as if he had forgotten that he was actually in a public place.

"Hello," he said, with the slightest hint of a smile around his perfect lips. Oh god. The liquor was making me horny too.

"Are you really reading Marquis de Sade?" I said, nodding at the book in his hands, *Philosophy in the Bedroom*. He laughed, looking at the book as if a little embarrassed.

"Yeah, ahh," he shrugged. "Classes start tomorrow. I have to study up. You're familiar with de Sade?"

"I've read some of his short fiction," I said. "He's one seriously twisted fuck."

That got him to laugh. I liked the way his eyes lit up when he did. He was nodding in agreement. "Yeah, I still haven't quite been able to get through *120 Days of Sodom*. Just so disturbing. But I find libertine philosophy, over all, to be pretty interesting-"

"Heeeeyyyy, giiiiirl!" Maya suddenly wrapped herself around me, hugging me way too tightly. Wow, she was drunk. She still had hunky-boy with her too. She motioned to him, "This is Rich, by the way. Oooh, and *hello*, who is this?"

"Adrian," he said, extending his hand to her. She looked confused, so he said his name again, louder this time. I don't think it actually did any good, because she called him Caitlyn for the rest of the night.

"Come on, we need more drinks," she said, tugging at me before her man-hunk shoved his way up to the bar. I really did not think I needed another drink. She definitely didn't need one. I looked back at Adrian a little helplessly.

"Do you want a drink?" I said.

He got up from his seat, tucking the book under his arm. "Shouldn't I be asking you that? I'll buy."

Maya was downing some pink thing with a cherry in it. Man-hunk was asking her if she could tie a knot in a cherry stem with her tongue. Now that he was standing, I realized how tall this Adrian guy was. He wasn't muscular, but he was well-built, slim and long. Like a pianist, or a painter, or something romantic like that. God. I really didn't need another drink.

"I'll get an Old Fashioned," Adrian said, before turning to me. "What would you like?"

"Oh, same thing you're having." I was slurring. Dammit. He frowned.

"Are you sure?"

I wasn't. But I said I was.

My ability to form short term memories for the rest of the night was awful. I remember a lot of 80's songs playing. I remember discovering that Old Fashioned's tasted awful, so Adrian finished mine for me. I had some vague recollection of grinding on him to Def Leppard's *Pour Some Sugar On Me*.

Then we were on the sidewalk. My heels were in my hand because my feet hurt like hell and I was telling Adrian that I could just walk back to my apartment because it was only two blocks. Maya had gotten an Uber with man-hunk, but it didn't matter because I knew this city like the back of my hand and I could walk two blocks at 1 in the morning no problem.

Adrian got an Uber. "I'm not letting you out of my sight," he said, helping me get into the car without hitting my head.

"Good, I'm not letting *you* out of my sight," I said. I wasn't really sure how loud I was speaking. Adrian had this amused little smile on his face, but I still felt as if I should apologize. I hiccupped. "Sorry. Sorry, Adrian."

He looked genuinely concerned. "Why?"

I bent over in the seat. I considered vomiting but decided that wasn't a good idea. "I'm just so drunk," I muttered.

I heard him laugh. That made me happy. "I know. Don't worry about it."

By the time we had reached my apartment, I knew exactly what I wanted. "You're coming up, right?" I said, as the car pulled to the sidewalk. He shook his head quickly.

"That's not a good idea," he said, but he sounded as if he regretted saying it. "You're too drunk."

I frowned and shoved him gently. "I'm not. Come on. Come up. You have to at least see me to my apartment right?"

Adrian considered a moment. His eyes – dark, chocolate-y brown – were suddenly hard when they met mine. Almost . . . scary.

"If I go up there," he said slowly. "You're not really going to get any sleep."

I grinned, feeling a kid in a candy shop. I took his hand and pulled him along after me as we left the car. "Come on then. Sleep is overrated."

I had forgotten what a mess my apartment was. I really hoped Adrian wouldn't notice. Luckily, he noticed Charles instead, my fluffy white cat, and he paused to give him chin scratches. He was hot *and* he liked cats? God damn.

"Are you sure about this?" he said, after I had managed to get him as far as the living room and then had to sit down on the couch. "You're really drunk." He kept saying that. Annoying.

"You're drunk too," I said. I had unhooked his belt from his jeans, and yanked it out of the loops. I folded it over and snapped it, mock-threatening. "Have you been a bad boy?"

He leaned down, his arms on either side of me against the couch, looking down at me. "Oh, no, no, no. *You've* been a very naughty girl."

Oh. Heat blossomed deep within me. I would have dropped the belt if he hadn't held out his hand for it. I set it gently in his hands. Was he really . . . was he actually going to-?

"Hold out your hands," he said softly, his voice a command I could not disobey. I did as he said, watching in drunken mystification as he looped the belt around and formed a pair of cuffs around my wrists. Keeping a hold on the loose end, he pulled my bound hands above my head. I felt his hand shaking as he stroked along my chin.

"Is this still alright with you?" he said. "Because I really . . . really want to do bad things to you."

I didn't even hesitate. "You can do whatever you want."

The grin that spread across his face was so deliciously predatory. I felt like I shrunk under him, suddenly small and helpless, his willing victim. He took a few moments to just look at me, and to see the appreciation in his gaze made me glow.

"Hmm," he said, examining the cuffs. "Let's try something different."

He released the cuffs, setting the belt aside and crushing me in his arms, his lips finding mine in a deep, passionate kiss. I felt his teeth clip my lip and then his hand was tangled in my hair, holding my head back and baring my throat to a trail of nips and sucks on my tender skin. I was gasping, shaking at every touch. I imagined one of those dramatic Harlequin Romance book covers, and realized I felt how they looked.

He pulled down the zipper on my dress as he kissed me, slipping it off me with expert fingers. Again, the appreciation with which he looked over my body, lingering in all the right place, made me tingle. He hooked his finger under my panties, but didn't pull them down. He was biting his lip, as if he was struggling.

Suddenly he laid me back on the couch, standing above me with the belt in his hand. "Curl your legs up to your chest," he said. "And put your wrists together behind your thighs.

I was little confused, until I actually got in position and he began to cuff my hands again. I realized that in this position, all my most intimate parts were perfectly exposed to him, and I could do nothing to cover them with my hands bound. The feeling of tightness and bondage was driving me wild. I found myself whimpering before he even touched me.

He grinned, running his fingers up the back of my thighs. "Do you like this?"

"Y-yes," I stuttered. My panties were soaked, a desperate need making me ache and chasing away the drunken haze that had clouded my thoughts. "Adrian . . . please . . ."

He leaned over me, his face far from the inconspicuous library boy he had appeared as at the bar. "Please what?" he said, and I felt his fingers hook around my panties again. This time, however, he slipped them up and pressed part of them into my bound hands. "Hold these out of my way," he said. "And try not to be too loud."

He trailed kisses down my legs, his fingers caressing along my body. His mouth was so close I could hardly stand it. Goosebumps covered me. "Please . . ." I moaned again.

Suddenly his mouth was on me. His tongue caressed along every fold, teased along every overwhelmingly sensitive part, so that my whole body began to shudder and I threw my head back as I groaned at the pleasure. He alternated between gentle sucks and precision strokes with his tongue, building up such a heat in me that I felt ready to explode. I was panting, and felt as if I had to struggle just to stop the seemingly endless tease.

I felt him chuckle against me as I pulled at the belt. "You're so sensitive," he said. He rose off of me for a moment, his tongue licking over his lips. "You're delicious, Cass. Every time you squirm you get a little bit wetter."

I felt as if I should have blushed, but all the heat and blood in me was centered squarely between my legs. It was all I could think of. I wanted so badly to feel his tongue again. "More please," I whimpered, wiggling the little bit I could with how bound I was. It was so frustrating to not be able to touch him, even more so when he unbuttoned his shirt and tossed it aside, his porcelain skin peppered with a light trail of hair across his chest and in a happy trail to his groin. I felt his fingers dig into my thighs. The way he looked at me . . . *god*, it was like he wanted to eat me alive.

"I'm really trying to go easy on you, Cass," he said. "But all your begging is really making that difficult." He leaned down, and whispered. "I want to give you something to really beg about."

I felt his fingers trace along between my legs, slick with the wetness there. He circled my clit, pressed – and then was inside of me. I clenched my mouth shut tight against the scream of pleasure that wanted to come out, muffling it down to a desperate cry. My feet kicked uncontrollably. He had one hand on my chest, firmly holding me down, watching my face with rapt attention as he slowly caressed inside me with his finger. He pulled out, and then thrust in again, this time with two fingers. I squealed.

"Next time I'll do something about all this kicking of yours," he said. "I'll need to teach you how to hold still."

Next time. Holy crap.

His fingers kept thrusting in a tantalizingly slow, methodical rhythm, and then he took his other hand and began to tease my clit. Now every thrust was bringing a squeal out of me, and I felt myself getting unbearably closer . . . and closer . . .

The orgasm wracked my entire body. Every part of me clenched and I pressed my face desperately into the couch as I screamed. He cruelly, *unbearably,* thrust faster as I came, drawing out my scream with a surgeon's precision. Hearing my cry subsiding, he withdrew his fingers and slowly licked them, watching me as he did.

"*Fuck,* Adrian," I breathed. I couldn't even form coherent sentences. I could hardly breathe. I watched as he stood up from the couch and unbuttoned his jeans.

"That's exactly what I intend to do," he said. He paused suddenly, and said, "Do you have condoms? I wasn't exactly . . . prepared for this."

"Bedside drawer," I said, a little breathlessly and extremely impatient. He disappeared into the bedroom for a moment, and came back with the tiny blue packet in his hand.

He kicked off his jeans, and then his briefs. He was hard and ready, rolling the condom quickly over his tip. Any hopes I'd had of being untied for this were cast away when he positioned himself above me, and I felt the tip of that thick thing tease my opening.

"Ready?" he whispered. I moaned and nodded, then moaned even louder as he stretched me, my already sensitive muscles spasming at the sensation and I almost came again. His careful control and maddening patience when pleasuring me was gone: he thrust into me with an urgency that made me grit my teeth at combination of pain and pleasure. One hand he wrapped around my throat, stifling my air, and the other he continued to tease my clit. All I could do was lay there, crying out his name with increasing ecstasy, until I heard him moan and felt him press even deeper inside me as he climaxed.

"We should get you to bed," was the last thing I heard him say as he removed the belt from around my wrists. All the liquor, adrenaline, and raging hormones were catching up with me swiftly. I was only barely aware of him scooping me up in his arms before I was sleeping like a baby.

CHAPTER TWO

I woke up in the morning to my blaring alarm. I had to avoid the temptation to throw my phone across the room just to shut it up, my head pounding mercilessly at every ring. I moaned, rolled over, and stuffed my head under the pillow.

What day was it? What had even happened last night? Why, oh why, did I drink so much?

Then a whole mess of information rushed back to my poor, alcohol-soaked brain. The bar. Adrian. The belt. The way his tongue had . . . *oh, god*.

It was the first day of classes.

I tried to fling myself out of bed, but my head swam and I had to stop and stay sitting at risk of throwing up all over my carpet. Charles poked his head in the door with a little *mrrow?*, likely concerned that he had yet to get his breakfast this morning.

"Sorry, Charlie," I moaned, holding my aching head. Why had I even let Maya convince me to go out?

Then again, if she hadn't I wouldn't have run into Adrian. I wouldn't have brought him back to my apartment, and we wouldn't have . . . I got goose bumps at the memory. Damn. I had rarely managed to orgasm with Ethan. In fact, trying to cum during sex with him was more of a chore than it was worth and he had never seemed to care one way or another, so I had usually just faked it. But with Adrian . . . god *damn*, I couldn't have stopped myself if I had tried. It was like my body had been perfectly under his control. Just thinking of the way he had bound me up, helpless with my legs up and exposed to him, was actually getting me all hot and bothered again despite the horrible hangover.

And I had been too drunk to even get his number. Damn it.

That was when I noticed that my bedside table had been mysteriously cleared of mugs. Only a single glass of fresh water and a small hand-written note remained. I drank the water thankfully, draining all of it before I picked up the note.

I hope this helps with the headache.

Thanks for a great night.

If you want more like it (when I don't have whiskey-dick, ha), just text me anytime.

Adrian's phone number was scrawled at the bottom. My heart skipped a beat. *That* had been whiskey-dick? What the hell was he like normally then? I stuffed the note in my pocket to put in my phone later, knowing I was running out of time. I couldn't be late on the first day of classes.

One quick shower later and I was on my way to campus with a makeup-free face and my messy hair thrown up in a ponytail. I had put on a pair of stretchy skinny jeans for the first time in days and a loose white t-shirt. So much for being that super-prepared girl for the first day of class. I had tried really hard to be *that* girl my whole freshman year, and it had honestly been exhausting.

The campus was packed. There were easy-ups around every corner where eager smiling ASB members waited to direct nervous freshman around the massive campus. I was luckily already familiar with nearly every building except for the obscure computer science labs that were tucked in the far back corner. I luckily had time to grab a quick coffee at the Starbucks inside the library before dashing over to Advanced English Literature.

The auditorium was large, with seating for at least a hundred students. Blackwood University was known for its writing programs, so a good number of their student body (including myself) was involved in either a writing or English major. The seats were slowly being filled, and I paused at the top of the auditorium to figure out where I wanted to lay my claim for the rest of the semester.

"Hey Cass."

Oh no. No, no, no. It was Ethan, about to walk into the classroom. Even worse, he hadSophia with him. Gorgeous, absolutely-looked-ready-for-the-day, blonde, perky-breastedSophia. My stomach flipped over. I felt nauseous immediately.

"Hey," I said, my voice cracking. He brushed past me with a tight uncomfortable smile, and he and Sophia took seats at the very top of the auditorium. No way was I going to sit through this whole semester with them anywhere within my field of vision. I walked all the way down to the lowest row, and took a seat just to the right of the professor's desk. My hand shook as I tried to take a casual sip on my macchiato. I just had to ignore him.

Minutes ticked by and the auditorium was nearly filled, still with no sign of the professor. The conversation had begun to reach a crescendo of noise when a door slammed above, and "Good morning class!" quieted the talk down to mere murmurs.

"Sorry about my late arrival, I had a long night." Shoes tapped down the long auditorium steps. His voice sounded young, and strangely familiar. "I'm sure you all know the drill: one too many drinks and suddenly you're waking up in a stranger's apartment." That got a few chuckles from the crowd, including me. Who the hell was this guy? I turned, just as the professor reached the bottom of the stairs and proceeded to his desk.

Oh. No. Oh my god.

"With that being said, welcome to Advanced English Lit. I'm Adrian Blackwood, you can call me Mr. Blackwood, Adrian, I really don't care as long as it isn't "douchebag." I've been called that one few times."

More giggles. My mouth had dropped open and I couldn't seem to pick it back up off my desk. Adrian was dressed in grey slacks and a maroon collared shirt, his blonde hair combed but still loose and wavy. His eyes roamed over the classroom, surveying us, until they came to me.

He dropped his briefcase a little too hard on the desk. I snapped my mouth shut, wanting to melt under the desk. Adrian quickly made a point to look anywhere but at me.

"*Okay*," he said softly, hissing between his teeth. "We'll start off with a little icebreaker. Don't worry, I'm not going to be taking roll call, there's way too many of you in here. Let me just tell you a little bit about myself." He casually seated himself at the edge of the desk, and his eyes flickered over me again, then quickly away. I couldn't stop staring.

"As I said, my name is Adrian Blackwood. I graduated from right here at Blackwood majoring in English, and I am actually *still* a Blackwood student." He looked at me again, as if to make a point. "I'm now working towards my Masters, in hopes of becoming a professor fulltime. That being said, me teaching this class does count towards my graduation, so if you could all please be respectful of that and *not* mess it up for me." He gave one of his charming, half smiles. He had really worked the crowd. Just glancing to my left I could see the adoring looks some of the girls – and a couple of the guys – were giving him. My stomach squeezed again, but this time it was with a strange possessiveness.

What the *hell* was wrong with me? How had I managed to have kinky, mind-blowing sex with my professor? Not that I could have possibly known – when he had mentioned classes I had thought he meant classes he was *in*, not teaching!

It's not that bad Cass, get a grip, I thought. *He's still a student, he just happens to be going for a Masters. This isn't a big deal. This probably happens all the time.*

Yeah. To judge by those lusty, small smiles he was getting, I was *certain* it happened all the time.

"First day will be pretty straightforward," he said, going to his briefcase and pulling out a packet of papers. "We'll go over the syllabus, a few expectations of what we'll cover, and hopefully get you all out of here early. So pull out your syllabus, hopefully you all printed them out."

Of course I had printed out nothing. He noticed.

"If you didn't, please share with your neighbor." Oh god, every look he gave me was giving me flashbacks. That mouth had been on me, *inside me.* I squeezed my legs together, trying to ignore the thoughts. How could I manage to say his name without remembering how I screamed it in ecstasy? I couldn't even *look* at him! He was wearing the same belt he had used to bind my hands together while he-

Jesus Christ, Cass, concentrate!

I didn't concentrate for a single second. The class passed in a blur. It felt as if Adrian and I made awkward eye contact every other minute. Finally, he said we were wrapped up for the day and would see us on Wednesday. I hurriedly began stuffing my notebook in to my bag, when his shadow fell over me.

"Would you mind waiting after class, for just a bit?" he said, his voice soft. I just nodded dumbly, and sat there as he attended to the line of questions from waitlisted and over-eager students. When the classroom was finally empty, I approached his desk.

"You're . . . a *professor*?" I blurted, unable to control my shock any longer. He winced.

"I'm not exactly a professor yet," he said. He looked as nervous as I felt, and I realized that this really was a worse position for him. Teachers got fired for things like this.

"Look," he said. "I really am sorry. If I'd known . . . it doesn't matter. I'll do everything I can to help you get into another class."

"I . . . this is really the only class that will fit into my schedule," I said. We both stared for a few moments, at a loss. I shrugged. "I'll be fine. I don't mind, really. It'll be like last night never happened."

His dark eyes watched me carefully. "You're sure you're alright?"

"Definitely!" I said, with just a little too much cheerfulness. I wanted to dispel the tension desperately, and I really wanted to just be out of his presence so I could stop imagining him bending me over the desk.

He didn't seem convinced as he slowly clicked his briefcase shut. "Alright. If you're sure. I'll see you on Wednesday, Cassandra. Please don't forget the readings."

Or else what? was what I wanted to say, but I smothered the urge. *Bad, Cass! Stop it.*

"Readings, right, got it," I tried to make a smooth exit and almost tripped over the first stair. I felt his eyes on the back of my head the entire way up the stairs. It was only once I was finally outside the classroom that I felt like I could breathe again.

CHAPTER THREE

S o my professor was an insanely hot, kinky sex god. So what? No big deal. I could handle this. It would be like it never even happened.

Ha! Yeah right. Your panties are already wet.

Somehow I managed to get through the rest of the day without looking like a complete ditz in my classes. My other professors were perfectly normal, average, not-at-all-distracting people. At some point Maya texted me wanting all the "juicy details" from the previous night. I didn't know where to begin. I wasn't even sure I wanted to tell her.

What part could I tell her exactly? The part where I'd let some random guy from the bar tie me up and finger me? The part where I'd turned into an absolute quivering, orgasming mess at his hands? Or the part where it turns out that random guy from the bar was my professor?

I decided to play it cool.

Haha, not really much to tell. He got me an Uber home and that's it.

I really was stupid to think that would get her off my back.

Oh come oooooonnnn, Casszy! You can NOT tell me nothing happened??

I already knew she wasn't going to let up. I sighed, and shoved my phone back into my purse. As I did, my hand came in contact with Adrian's note. Seeing his neat handwriting made my heart pound. What kind of guy could be so absolutely dominating and down for sex with a stranger, and then nice enough to not only put my drunk ass to bed, but get me water for the morning? I suddenly remembered his words, "Next time I'll do something about all this kicking."

My insides quivered, but disappointment was settling in too. There wasn't going to be a "next time" now. I was just going to have to stare at this guy every Monday and Wednesday for the rest of the semester until I could permanently put him out of my thoughts.

Not only that, but I had to sit in that classroom with the knowledge that Ethan and his new girlfriend were sitting behind me, looking down at me. Of course, Ethan's first time seeing me after our breakup and I looked like my life was falling apart: no makeup, hair tangled, sick as a dog with this hangover. I was determined that next time I would show him *exactly* what he was missing out on. He thought I was weak? Oh, I'd make *him* weak.

The next morning Maya and I headed out with coffees in hand to the mall. I had managed to keep quiet about what had happened with Adrian, but I *had* told her about Ethan and Sophia being in my class. She had responded exactly as I hoped, in true Maya-fashion.

"What. A. Dick!" she had shrieked. "Oh my god. He is *the* biggest asshole."

"Which is why I need to get something new," I said. "You know, show him what he's missing."

"Ooo, new Cass the heartbreaker," Maya said, squirming excitedly. "I like it!"

It was relieving to feel my heartbreak patching itself up with anger, even if somewhere deep inside I knew that was not going to work in the long run. For now, the whole concept of a revenge glow-up sounded really appealing. I even thought about getting a gym membership.

Thought about, and then quickly changed my mind, my excuse being that Charles was alone enough as it was. I kept catching glimpses of a Crazy Cat Lady future for myself if I didn't stop using Charles as an excuse for things.

Once in the mall, I went for all the pieces I loved that I usually would have avoided because of Ethan's disapproval. The tight little black numbers that reminded me of my emo high school days, when I would listen to Bring Me the Horizon and My Chemical Romance on loop. Strappy shirts, tight skirts, dark painted-on jeans. I guess at my age I should have probably been shopping for blazers and button-ups, but there was a certain power in reclaiming a style that had always made me feel powerful, mysterious, and slightly frightening.

Our last stop was Victoria's Secret. As Maya wandered off to the Pink section, I slyly snagged a few corsets and lingerie sets, even knowing they were too expensive. Who would I wear them for anyway? Myself? Even so, as I stood in the perfectly-lit fitting room and looked at myself in the massive mirror, I liked what I saw. My ass was more of a pancake than a birthday cake, but hey, who didn't like pancakes anyway? I actually felt . . . beautiful.

I snapped a few pictures with my phone before changing back into my regular clothes, deciding to just take the hit and pull out my credit card for once. The lingerie would just be for me and Charles to enjoy.

Adrian's phone number was an itch I couldn't scratch. I had his note in my hand three times to throw away, only to put it back on the countertop each time. Finally, exasperated, I sat down on the couch with his note in one hand and my phone in the other.

I knew I shouldn't. It just wasn't appropriate. But what if I hadn't happened to be put in his class? I could have gotten any of the other classes if my schedule had fit, and I would have texted him already.

A sudden smell made me tingle. The couch still smelled like his cologne, a dark musky scent that made me think of old libraries and leather.

God. Dammit.

I put his number into my phone and typed up a quick message.

So I know that we're going to act like the other night didn't happen, but I felt rude not thanking you for such a fun night ;)

I attached one of the pictures I had taken in the fitting room, the one that made my ass look the least pancake-y. Before I could change my mind, I clicked *send* and then promptly flung the phone to the other end of the couch.

"What's wrong with me, Charles?" I said, as he looked at me with wide yellow eyes.

The phone buzzed. *Oh god, oh god, oh god.* With a deep breath I picked it up and swiped the unlock screen.

In light of last night never having happened, who is this and how did you get this number?

Also, pictures like that are naughty. Pictures like that get pretty little asses like yours spanked.

I practically squealed, giggling to myself. Naughty indeed. He had actually threatened to *spank* me. I had always secretly liked the idea, but had never felt comfortable asking Ethan for something like that. It looked like I'd just have to keep being a naughty girl then.

The phone buzzed again.

Fuck.

Please forget I sent that.

We shouldn't be in contact like this.

Too late for that, Professor Adrian Blackwood.

CHAPTER FOUR

I arrived on campus the following day with Marilyn Manson blasting on my headphones. His music was so nostalgic; once again, hearkening back to my 14-year-old, weirdo self. What kind of almost-quarter-life crisis was I going through with this crap? To be fair, the music also served as a great distraction from the stares I was getting. I might have overdone my "revenge" clothing. The black collared dress I was wearing was a little Wednesday Addams-esque, and now that I thought about it, the sheer thigh-highs were *definitely* too much. I hid my discomfort with my own attention-attracting appearance behind massive black sunglasses.

I did feel a little bit better as I found myself approaching the classroom just ahead of Ethan. I tossed my hair back, but on my best resting bitch face, and strutted into the auditorium just ahead of him. The look of absolute shock on his face was *priceless.*

Don't fall, don't fall, don't fall, I thought as carefully made my way down the stairs.

Adrian was on time today, already sitting at his desk sipping a coffee as the students filed in. He caught sight of me immediately.

Oh my god. His face. He put down his coffee cup carefully, his expression the same one I had seen on his face when he had crouched over me on the couch that night. Predatory. Like he would eat me alive. Suddenly Ethan seemed extremely unimportant.

I sat quietly in my seat at the front of the room, almost wishing that someone else had claimed it so I could have been forced to choose a less obvious seat further back. I crossed my legs, even though I knew it made one heeled foot stick out tantalizingly. Adrian was shooting me fiery looks, and I honestly could not tell if he was mad or entertained.

Adrian flicked off the lights, and the projector lit up the white board with a painting of Marquis de Sade. "Good morning class. I hope you all enjoyed your first reading. How many of you here were already familiar with de Sade?"

Several hands shot up across the room, including mine. I could have sworn I saw Adrian's mouth twitch in a small grin when he saw my hand go up. "Very good. So who can tell me a bit about him?"

"He really liked sex!" shouted a male voice. There were a few snickers and murmurs of agreement. Adrian smiled.

"He did," he said. "Marquis de Sade, like another famous writer you may be familiar with, Mr. John Wilmot, was a libertine. Libertines had a very particular philosophy that even today would probably be considered rather unusual, let alone during their time. Can anyone tell us a bit about the Libertine philosophy?"

"They didn't believe in boundaries," I said. "They believed there shouldn't be any restraints to how one lives their lives, whether sexual or moral. They placed a strong value on physical pleasures, the stimulation of the senses."

"Very good, Miss Cassandra," Adrian's gaze lingered on my nylon-clad leg for just a moment longer than it should have, eliciting the most delicious little rush of excitement from me. "In fact, this perverse approach to sexuality that Marquis de Sade had is part of the reason we have the word "sadism" today: it's actually based off of his name."

I was feeling pleased with myself by the time class had ended. I'd disarmed my ex and Adrian hadn't stopped giving me lingering looks the entire class. Still, the heels were starting to get just a little painful, and I considered going back to my apartment in between classes to get a more comfortable pair of shoes. The heels had already served their purpose for the day anyway.

As I was collecting my things to leave, Adrian called to me from his desk, "Cassandra, could I have a word with you?"

My insides shuddered excitedly. "Yes, professor?" I said, putting a little more emphasis on *professor* than I really needed to. He remained seated at his desk, hands folded in front of him in a way that seemed dangerously patient.

When he spoke, his voice was low. "What exactly are you trying to do to me, Miss Cassandra?"

I feigned confusion. "I'm not sure what you mean, Mr. Blackwood."

He exhaled loudly through his nose. "You know exactly what I mean. The picture? Really? And this . . . these clothes?"

I laughed softly. "I don't think you can tell me how to dress, professor."

He got up from his chair, slowly. There were still a few students leaving the room, so he leaned closer and kept his voice down as he said, "I wouldn't tell you how to dress, Cass. I would love to see you dress like this every day. That's the problem. Because seeing you like this makes me want to do bad things to you. Things that, as your professor, I'm morally obligated not to do."

Inside, I was absolutely writhing. On the outside, I shrugged. "Maybe you should take a page out of Libertine philosophy, Mr. Blackwood. Dispose of the boundaries."

His jaw clenched. "Don't tempt me."

"Or what?" I said dangerously. The classroom was empty. I turned to go. Let him think that little exchange over. Let *him* be the one obsessing over *me*. It felt good to be the powerful one for a change, after Ethan had spent so much time bringing me down.

"Cassandra!" The sharpness is his voice made me stop. I glanced back over my shoulder. He was seated back in his chair, fiery-eyed and loosening his tie. "Get back over here, and get over my knee."

My eyes widened. "W-what?"

"You heard me," his voice was commanding, irresistible. "Get back here. *And get over my knee.*"

CHAPTER FIVE

I stood there frozen. I was suddenly tingly everywhere, heat swelling within me. I kept expecting him to grin and admit it was a joke. But he looked dead serious. Was he actually going to spank me in the classroom?

I walked back to him, slowly, cautiously. What kind of spanking was he talking about here? Like those little love pats you occasionally saw in super vanilla porn, or like creepy-side-of-the-web, debatably consensual Russian porn where the girls ended up bruised? Standing in front of him, I smiled nervously.

"You're really going to spank me?" I said, a little tremble in my voice.

"Yes, I am," he said, beginning to roll up the sleeve on his right arm. The motion made my insides clench. "Are you going to accept your punishment?"

I hesitated. I could still walk out the door. But I didn't want to. I was curious. I wanted that feeling again, that feeling I'd had tied up on my own couch, used and exposed.

I stepped forward in acquiescence. The moment I did, he grabbed hold of my wrist and pulled me down so that I was lying across his lap. My head hung down, and my bottom was positioned just at the edge of his thigh. My dress was short enough that the moment I was bent over, I could feel that my panties were exposed. I gasped sharply, my first instinct to push myself back up, but his hand on my back held me down.

"Hold still, little girl," he said. *Oooh, god.* My thighs trembled as lust swelled in me. There it was, that delicious feeling of helplessness, of smallness, just like I had felt when I was tied up on my own couch, forced to cum on his fingers. His hand brushed over my ass, caressed my black silk panties and gently traced beneath each cheek. I doubted that gentleness would last long.

"Try not to be too loud," he said, echoing a command I'd heard before. "We wouldn't want someone to come in and see you like this, now would we?"

The very idea of someone coming in to see me bent over my professor's lap, bottom exposed beneath my short skirt, about to be spanked, made my cheeks burn. The cheeks on my face that is, but I was certain my lower cheeks would be burning soon enough too.

"I think it's important to understand why you're going to be punished," Adrian said. I could hear the smile in his voice. God, he was enjoying this. He continued to caress my skin, over each cheek and even down my thighs. "Do you know why I'm about to spank you, Miss Cass?"

I began shaking my head like a petulant child, although I probably could have guessed the "why." Adrian chuckled, and before I realized what he was doing, he had swung down his hand with a sharp slap across my ass.

"Aahh!" I cried out before I could stop myself, and then quickly pressed my lips together. Dammit, that hurt. The sting lingered even as his hand went back to caressing me. Almost immediately, as if he had slapped some kind of "on" button, my desire increased.

"I'm spanking you because you're trying to make things difficult for me, even after I told you it would be inappropriate to continue contact outside of the classroom," Adrian said, sounding so controlled, so reasonable. "I'm spanking you because you seem to think you want to keep up some kind of relationship with me outside of what should be a very chaste professor-student relationship." Another spank. This time I managed to muffle myself down to a whimper. "I'm spanking you because you need to be aware of what exactly you're asking to be involved in."

He spanked me again, and again, faster now as he stopped talking and seemed to be solely concentrating on making my ass burn. Every slap was bringing a whimper out of me, and it was getting harder and harder to keep myself quiet. My legs were shaking, my breath coming in gasps and I began to moan in between sharp, pained whimpers. The parts of my cheeks that were exposed at the edges of my panties felt as if they had been gone over with sand paper, and every time his hand slapped those tender places my cries increased in volume until I finally let out a desperate, pained, "Please Adrian!"

He paused. "Please what, Miss Cassandra? Are we done?"

"Yes!" I said quickly, my voice trembling. Somehow I didn't really want to leave his lap. That vulnerable position had me going absolutely mad.

"Oh really?" he said musingly. His hand stroked over my surely reddened skin, squeezing it here and there and making me gasp. "You don't think you deserve anymore?"

I couldn't answer that. The little voice inside me was savagely screaming, "More!" But my body felt as if it had reached its limit. If he kept going, I wouldn't be able to control my volume.

When I didn't answer other than to whimper softly, he pulled me up and helped me to my feet. I immediately felt the desire to cover my face with my hands. I could feel myself blushing furiously. He straightened my dress, pulling it back down to cover me. He stood, and tenderly took my face in his hands.

"Did you like that?" he whispered. Without hesitation, I nodded in the affirmative. A smile spread across his beautiful lips, the kind of devilish grin that made me want to rip his clothes off.

"Next time," he promised softly. "I'll take off your panties and have you hold them in your mouth to muffle all that whimpering."

Oh my god. I wanted him desperately, the ache in me completely unbearable. But he stepped away, and sat back down at his desk.

"You're dismissed, Miss Cassandra," he said, his knowing grin telling me that he was well aware of how in need I was. "I'll see you next class."

"Please don't make me wait that long," I whispered, almost whining. He raised his eyebrows in surprise.

"We'll see," he said carefully. "I think for now you have other classes to attend to, don't you?"

"Yes, professor," I said, and despite my thoroughly chastised state I allowed myself a cheeky little grin as I collected my things and left the auditorium.

CHAPTER SIX

Feeling my skin sting in every seat I had for the rest of the day was a very particular kind of torture. I couldn't get Adrian's calm, dominating voice out of my head. I knew now that there was no going back. I had to have more of him.

My phone buzzed as I was getting into my apartment that night, and I pulled it eagerly out of my purse. Seeing Ethan's name on my screen made my heart skip a beat, and not in a good way.

Glad to see you doing well Casszy :) I hope you know I'll always be here for you.

I was instantaneously irritated. What the hell was *that* supposed to mean? He had barely even been there for me when we were together. I texted back quickly, as Charles rubbed around my feet, demanding food.

I don't thinkSophia would appreciate you texting your ex. Take it from a girl who's been there.

Satisfied that he wasn't going to get me to give in to his cheesy lines, I fed Charles before pouring myself a glass of wine and settling onto the couch to watch Game of Thrones. I was only 10 minutes into an episode before my phone buzzed again. It was still Ethan.

Don't worry,Sophia is super chill. She wouldn't mind if we were still friends.

I laughed aloud, making Charles look up at me skeptically from his food bowl. Even though it made me laugh, I was shaking with anger. Friends? Really? After all his shit, after the cheating, the lying, the cruel words, breaking me down one underhanded comment at a time?

Fuck off Ethan. We're not friends. We'll never be friends.

I threw down my phone, determined to be done with it. It buzzed again almost immediately. I didn't want to pick it up. I didn't want to know what he had to say. I didn't want to give him the chance to get inside my head.

I picked up the phone.

You're overthinking, as usual Cass. Just because I didn't want to commit my whole life to you doesn't mean you have to be a bitch. But whatever. I guess you'll just go on being miserable with yourself.

I deleted the text thread, my hands shaking. I really tried not to cry. But furious tears were making my eyes sting and my chest hurt. For a few brief seconds, I buried my face in my hands and let go, hard sobs wracking my chest. I hated him. *Hated* him. I wanted to change my phone number, block him, erase every trace of him from existence. I wanted to forget all the things he had ever said to make me feel bad about myself, things that wheedled their way deep into my brain because I'd been stupidly vulnerable and in love.

My phone buzzed again. From where it lay face up on the cushion, I could see that it wasn't Ethan this time.

It was Adrian.

I scrubbed the tears off my face and picked it up.

I was just thinking of you. Are you okay?

I almost started crying again, just from relief. Why did I have to be so emotional? Sniffling, I texted him back.

I'm trying to be. Hard night.

Almost immediately, his response:

Do you need to talk?

My heart swelled, and then immediately fell. I didn't want to involve him in my drama already. What guy would want to stick around a girl who was still crying over her ex? Better to keep it as simple as possible than have Adrian think I was weak too.

Thank you, but I'll be okay. I just need a little time and to finish my glass of wine, haha.

A minute passed, and then:

Cass, if we're going to keep doing this incredibly stupid thing that I know we both want, we need to keep communication as open as possible. Are you sure you don't need to talk?

I smiled, his concern touching me.

No, really, it's okay. Just not tonight. I'm too emotional I guess. Hormones or some shit.

I waited. Then:

Please don't write off your feelings. Whatever you feel right now is valid. It's alright if you don't want to talk tonight, but please soon. Would you be free to come to my house Saturday night for dinner?

Woah . . . did he mean a date? An actual date? I hesitated before responding. The amazing sex was one thing, but a date meant emotions. It meant more of these crappy feelings that were currently making me heart feel like it was getting punched. *Open communication.* I guess there couldn't be any harm.

Sure thing. I'll be free :)

As I lay in bed that night, my mind was rushing. Was I really about to get this deeply involved? When Adrian said "open communication," surely he didn't *really* want to hear what was going on inside my head. The insecurity, the uncertainty, the rushing thoughts. No guy wanted to hear that. Still, Adrian had so far not been like any other man I had been involved with. Not only because of the kinky sex, but because of the care he took in every interaction with me. The questions. The way he watched my face for acceptance and hesitation.

I tossed and turned, disturbing Charles and making him run

off to sleep on the couch. It was just dinner . . . and probably sex. *God, yes please.* Now that I had calmed down from what Ethan had said, I was still aching from earlier. My ass stung against my pajama pants, and I finally had to slip out of them to be more comfortable. With my eyes closed, I thought of the way Adrian's eyes had looked as he called me over to him.

"Come here, little girl, and get over my knee."

The touch of my own fingers between my legs made me shudder. I imagined Adrian's fingers caressing inside me: the way they had found every tender, sensitive spot and manipulated it fully. I moaned softly, imagining him above me, his hand squeezing my throat with perfect control. My pleasure peaked and I gasped, shuddering. The rush forced the anxiety from my body, and I rolled over, exhausted. With sleep swiftly consuming me, my last lingering thought was of Adrian's gentle, dangerous hands caressing my face as he whispered,

"Did you like that?"

I managed to throw myself into catching up on my reading for the next several days. I took careful notes, highlighted passages and tagged pages, determined to get my head in the right place. If I was going to go into a lifetime of debt with student loans, I was going to at least make it worth my while with good grades.

I worked part time in the campus bookstore, so in between study sessions I spent the rest of my hours there. I was falling back in to a strange and unfamiliar normalcy with Ethan out of my life. I had gotten so used to spending my free time after working studying with him at his mom's house that I was uncertain at first what to do with those hours. I spent way more time than was really necessary compiling reading notes and making my notebooks look aesthetically appealing with multi-colored gel pens. I was slowly learning to be myself again.

Then, far sooner than I expected, I was waking up on Saturday. It didn't hit me at first, and then I remembered: today was the day. I was going to Adrian's house for dinner.

I spent most of the day in restless anxiety. I cleaned the entire house, threw out old food in the fridge, and even began raiding my closet and throwing out the worn out clothes I didn't wear anymore. My nervousness was suspended between two ideas: the first was my worry over actually having to sit down and have an intimate conversation with someone new. Adrian made me feel comfortable, open. But our engagement had never gone beyond the realm of tense flirting and dark sexual encounters. What if he wanted more than I was ready for? He was a little older than me, so what if he was one of those commitment-ready types who drew out timelines for their relationships and set deadlines on when they should be married by?

The other idea was less a worry and more a giddy, nervous excitement. I was going into Adrian's territory now, and after all his promises of what he would do to me "next time," I could hardly bear the wait. Especially after getting no release from him after that spanking in the classroom. I could get myself off, sure. But for the first time I had found a guy who could give me more pleasure than I could give myself. Thoughts of him kept me tense throughout the day, until I managed to distract myself getting ready to leave.

My phone buzzed, a text from him.

Still on for tonight? Here's my address.

It was for an apartment on the other side of town, a nicer area located near yoga studies and juice bars. I threw on a dark violet dress, a slim leather choker and a pair of patent leather pumps. As a final, devilish touch, I made sure to wear the new black garter belt and thong I had sent him a picture of previously. My nerves were shaking me up even more as I went to the parking garage to fetch my car. This wasn't a big deal. It was only a big deal if I *made* it a big deal. It was just a nice, simple, ground-rule laying talk over dinner.

I texted him my arrival after I had parked. The apartment building he lived in was tall and modern, a nice combination of red brick and brushed steel. There were plenty of people meandering the streets on a Saturday night, popping in the various bars and cafes. Unlike downtown, the bars here attracted a slightly older, calmer crowd. There was an actual apartment lobby and a doorman who directed me to the elevators. I entered and pushed the button for the 9th floor.

My phone buzzed.

Let yourself in, the door is unlocked :) I'm just finishing up dinner.

He was actually cooking for me? My stomach growled and I realized that I hadn't eaten anything since early that morning when I had slurped down a single bowl of cereal. Stepping out of the elevator, I found his apartment at the very end of the hall. I checked my lipstick a final time, and with an irrational fear that I was about to barge into the wrong person's apartment, I opened the door.

The smell of something heavenly filled the air, spicy and savory. The entryway turned immediately to the right, leading me by a slim decorative table topped with some odd silver art piece that looked like a ball of crunched metal.

"Hello? Adrian?"

"In here!" his voice echoed from just at the end of the hall. I peered around the corner, and found myself looking into an open style kitchen. Everything was sleek, modern, and compact, a relatively small space that Adrian seemed to have taken full advantage of. He was standing there over a sizzling pan of what look like creamy pasta. I smiled immediately. There was no more sure-fire way to make me happy than with carbs.

"I hope you like Scoglio," he said, with an easy smile. He wasn't wearing his glasses this time, so his dark eyes caught me even more intensely as they turned to me. He was dressed casually, in a black short-sleeved button-up with dark jeans. I couldn't help wondering if he was wearing his belt today. His hair was loose, giving him the appearance that he had just been running through wheat fields, or surfing on the California coast.

Wow, Cass, stop staring at the man and say something human.

"Smells great!" I said, squeaking in my eagerness. He chuckled as he took the pan off the burner and began to scoop the pasta and seafood goodness onto two plates. He had a small table just beyond the kitchen, at which point the dining area led to an open living room. All his furniture was varying tones of greys and dark blues, and it was peculiarly clean for a bachelor pad. There was a modestly-sized flat screen on the wall, so clearly this guy wasn't surviving off of mere student wages. Off to the right was a closed door, leading to what I assumed was the bedroom.

"I heard you like wine?" I turned, to see that Adrian had already set the table and was holding a wine bottle. He popped the cork and began to pour, the blood-red liquid filling our glasses. "I'll be honest, I know a lot more about whiskey than I do about wine. But the woman at the store said this was a good one, so . . ." He shrugged, looking rather sheepish. It was fascinating to see him outside of his usual dominant state. Even so, just being near him was giving me pleasant little shivers.

"I hope your other classes have been a little less . . . unusual . . . than mine," he said as we ate. I was trying to eat slowly and not like a starving animal, but the food was delicious. I dabbed my mouth carefully with my napkin before answering. So much for my lipstick lasting long.

"No, I have to say your class is the only one I feel like I'll be getting extra credit for," I smiled slyly, happy to get a laugh out of him.

"Oh, I see how it is," he said. "I should have known, it's all just for the extra credit."

"A girl has to graduate somehow."

We both laughed easily. My anxiety had entirely dispersed,

replaced with an overwhelming curiosity, a desire to hear him speak.

"Where did you learn to cook like this?" I said.

"Well, my mom is full-blooded Italian," he said. "And I mean straight-from-Italy Italian. She was in the kitchen every night cooking for us, so of course all the kids had to learn to cook."

"All the kids? How many of you are there?"

"I'm the second oldest," he said, taking a sip on his wine as if trying to remember exactly how many siblings he had. "My brother Damien is oldest. My sisters Elaina and Adrianna are youngest, they're twins."

"Damn, four kids," I said. "My parents just had us two, my brother and I."

He chuckled, "Yeah, family reunions are always fun, especially considering that the only one of us who still adheres to Catholicism is Adrianna. My poor mom just about had a heart attack when I told her I was an atheist." He shook his finger and mimicked a high-pitched voice. "My son, you are going to straight to Hell! I will pray for you!" He shook his head. "And don't even get me started on how horrified she was that I was actually going to move out to go to school."

"My mom couldn't wait to have us out of the house," I said, still smiling at the idea of a small Italian woman scolding Adrian for his lack of religion. "She was the typical white suburban soccer mom. But after she and dad split up, I think she really just wanted to get back into the dating scene. Feel like she was 20 again, or something like that. She couldn't really feel 20 with two kids in the house."

Adrian nodded in understanding. We traded stories, laughing about Adrian's father catching him smoking pot at 13, or the time my mother had walked in on me watching PornHub. We talked about the many places I had lived growing up since my father was in the military, and that I planned to try to study abroad in Europe.

"If you stay in Italy, I can set you up with family there," Adrian said. "They'll do nothing but feed you the entire time."

I helped him clear the dishes before we sat down to another glass of wine. The view of the city through his windows was stunning: the lights twinkling and neon bar signs flickering. The conversation lulled and Adrian's gaze went over my face, searching.

"So," he said, leaning his chin on his hand. "What are you looking for Cass? With what we're doing . . . what kind of relationship do you want?"

I squirmed. I wasn't used to being asked so frankly about something as simple as what I wanted from a man. It should have been simple, but I found myself stuttering.

"I'll be honest, Adrian," I said, with a little sigh. "I just got out of a relationship. Two years. My ex really put me through shit, and I'm not . . . I'm just not really . . ."

"Ready for a relationship?" he finished for me.

I shrugged. I felt guilty. "Yeah. My emotions aren't in the right place."

"That's fine," he said, smiling when he noticed my obvious discomfort. "Don't feel bad to say what you want and don't want, Cass. It's important. I have no problem with something casual."

"I like what you do to me," I said softly. "This whole . . . dominance thing. I really like that."

He chuckled darkly. "I noticed. You're definitely a submissive."

Worry suddenly punched me in the gut. Submissive. Weak, like Ethan had said. Trying too hard and getting walked all over. I swallowed hard.

"You don't like that term?" Adrian frowned slightly, immediately intuitive to my discomfort. I shrugged again.

"It's just that my ex always told me I was too . . . too weak. That I let him walk all over me and do what he wanted." *Crap.* My eyes were actually welling up with tears. "And I did, honestly. Like I knew he was cheating and I still . . . tried to make it work."

Adrian's frown deepened. "You can't blame yourself for that. And being submissive isn't weak. It takes a great deal of trust and effort to submit to your partner. The fact that your ex abused your trust is *his* weakness, not yours." He tapped his fingers on the tabletop. "Are you familiar with BDSM relationships? Was your ex-"

"He really didn't care what happened during sex as long he got off," I scoffed. "I've never actually had someone make me orgasm like you did."

He smiled, looking pleased with himself. "I'm glad. It pleases me to please you. Perhaps that sounds odd coming from someone who, very obviously, is pretty sadistic."

I laughed. "Oh you mean you actually *liked* spanking me? I thought it hurt you as much as it hurt me."

He chuckled darkly. "I thoroughly enjoyed every second of you whimpering and trying to stay quiet. I liked watching your skin get red and knowing that each spank got progressively worse for you. And there are many other painful things I would enjoy doing to you, Cass. But what is very important about this is that if we continue this relationship – even casually – is that you must understand that as the submissive, you hold the power."

I frowned, confused. "Isn't that . . . like the exact opposite of the whole BDSM thing?"

"Not at all. It's crucial that the sub, or submissive, maintains the authority of the last word. If you need me to stop, I will stop. The idea is that the submissive wants these things – punishments, domination, bondage, humiliation - just as much as the dominant does. So obviously you would push your own boundaries, and have the trust in me to stop when you need me to."

I had never thought of it that way. I honestly knew next to nothing about the BDSM scene and what it entailed, besides the whole whips and chains part. It seemed Adrian was more experienced.

"You've had submissives before?" I queried.

"I have," he said. "Every relationship I've had so far in my adult life incorporated elements of BDSM. It's simply what I enjoy, and what I know I need to be satisfied. What all that incorporates depends entirely on who I'm with and what they like. I have very few hard limits myself. I'm open to almost anything."

Hard limits. I hadn't thought about that before either. Then again, with my limited knowledge, there were only so many things I could think of as being immediately opposed to.

"I mean . . . I would prefer if we didn't do anything related to golden showers," I said with a shrug. He laughed aloud, shaking his head.

"That's fine with me," he said. "Is there anything else you're opposed to? Or better yet, is there anything you want to try?"

My mind was becoming a blank, filled with rushing thoughts and a growing horniness. Was I really sitting here discussing the intricacies of a BDSM relationship with my professor? Was I really discussing *being in* a relationship? My heart jumped, nervousness stifling me. Adrian noticed.

"You're worried," he said. "Why?"

I shook my head. "I just . . . I have a lot of baggage, Adrian. Most of the time I don't feel strong, like you say a sub should be. I don't always feel pretty, or desirable. I got left after two years for a girl who was doing everything I was too scared to do. I really . . . I just . . ."

"You don't want to get hurt," he said softly. I nodded. He sighed, but not in an irritated way. He almost sounded sad. Then he looked up, and those dark eyes met mine with the vicious intensity that made my insides immediately clench.

"Come into the bedroom," he said. "Let me show you how strong you are."

The bedroom was dark, dominated by a massive four-poster bed. The sheets and coverlet were all silky greys and reds. A window took up the wall to our left, and Adrian moved ahead of me to throw back to the curtains, lighting the room in the city's neon glow. The opposite wall was dominated by three large bookshelves, covered with literature from end to end.

"That's an impressive collection," I said softly. Adrian smiled, taking my hand and leading me nearer to the bed. He pulled me close in his arms, and I surrendered to the embrace. His fingers caressed up my throat, stopping to take gentle hold of my face.

"Remember," he said. "Trust me to be in control, but don't be afraid to tell me to stop. I'm going to push you, Cass. I want to see how far your limits are."

I nodded, desire spreading through me and making my skin tingle. The naughty voice inside was screaming for his touch, for him to throw me down on the bed and have his way with me. But to judge from the diabolical way his eyes were gleaming as he moved behind me to unzip my dress, I had a feeling it was not going to be that easy.

"I am going to discipline your desire," he said, his fingers stroking my back as his opposite hand drew my zipper down. Goose bumps spread over my skin. His lips brushed my neck – once, twice – and then his teeth found a hold at the sensitive spot between my neck and shoulder. I whined softly. His hands drew the shoulders of my dress down over my arms, and then down past my waist.

"Mmm, I recognize this lingerie," he said. "You tempted me with these things before." His hands grasped my hips appreciatively then reached down to cup my ass. He squeezed, and I felt his fingers trace along the thong. "What did I warn you about wearing things like this? Naughty things like this will get your pretty little ass spanked."

I gasped as I felt him bend down and nip at my exposed cheek. He kissed along my bottom, his hand holding my hips in place as his teeth grabbed me again. I didn't know what to do with my hands as he continued to send chills running over my body. I wanted to tangle my fingers in his hair and pull him close. I wanted to feel his tongue.

He suddenly turned me around, jerking me close to him with his hands still squeezing my ass. "Someday soon," he said, holding me captive me his gaze. "I'm going to claim your ass as mine. I'll fill that tight little hole with every inch of me."

My eyes widened. Now *that* was something I had never done before. The idea of being invaded *there*, somewhere so tight and somehow even more intimate, made my toes curl. My breath caught as Adrian suddenly pushed me back onto the bed, the soft blankets swallowing me. I gasped again when he seized hold of my arms, expertly flipping me over onto my stomach so that I was bent over the edge of the tall bed. His nails traced down my back, hooked under my panties and swiftly yanked them down.

"Listen carefully, little girl," he said. One hand was pressed against the small of my back, while the other was playing tantalizingly below my cheeks. "If you beg me to stop, I won't. We'll use a safety word. That way you can more fully engage in your submission to me. What safety word would you prefer?"

"Uh . . ." I couldn't think. Every inch of me was hot and bothered and the last thing I could come up with was a word that would make him stop the very thing that was making me this way. He chuckled, seemingly aware of my predicament.

" "Red" is typically my go-to," he said. "So remember that. If you really need me to stop, if you are no longer enjoying yourself and it becomes too much for you, that's what you'll say."

"Okay," I breathed, then immediately yelped. His hand had swatted down across my bare backside, leaving a stinging space the size of his hand.

"We're going to fix how you address me," he said. "As your dominant, I will expect you to address me with the proper respect. "Yes, sir," and "no, sir" are appropriate responses. Do you understand?"

"Oka- I mean yes, sir!" I had felt his hand cock back for

another swat. Instead it went back to gently caressing me as I corrected myself. I sighed, all my pent up adrenaline and desire make my head spin.

"Already so eager for me," he said with a little chuckle, as one finger teasingly stroked over my most intimate place. "You're going to have to wait quite a while for that little girl. I'm going to make you suffer for me first. Remember what I told you after your last spanking?"

I couldn't seem to remember. I was too wound up, too utterly absorbed in his voice to think back on anything else. "I don't remember, sir."

"I told you that next time I spanked you, I would make you hold your own panties in your mouth to keep quiet."

Oh. I remembered now. I could still feel my panties around my ankles. "W-why are you going to spank me, sir?" I said. "I . . . I've been good right?"

He laughed, and I felt him tug the panties off completely. "You knew what you were doing when you wore this thong and garter over here. You're a smart girl, I know you remembered what I said to you about them last time. What kind of master would I be if I didn't hold to my word and discipline you for wearing something so naughty? So open wide."

I hesitated, and then opened my mouth. Almost immediately I felt the silky fabric of my thong pushed into my mouth. My first instinct was revulsion, to spit it out. The humiliation of having my own underwear shoved in my mouth made me squirm. But it also felt delicious. I felt helpless, obedient. I didn't want to stop. I held the panties in my mouth, resigned. Submissive.

"Good girl," Adrian said, leaning over my back to whisper in my ear. He tucked my hair back behind my ear, his thumb tracing along my jawline. "You look beautiful." Pride and pleasure glowed inside me. "Now hold still for me. I'm not going to go easy on you this time."

Easy on me? Had he gone easy on me last time? I didn't have the time to consider it before the first swat fell, and then another and another in rapid succession. Before long I was squirming desperately, squealing against the panties in my mouth with each spank. My skin was burning, every inch of my body tingling with stimulation.

Just when I began to be convinced I would have to tell him I couldn't take anymore, he stopped. I lay there trembling, letting out shaking muffled sighs as I tried to compose myself. His hand rubbed over my stinging skin as he moaned appreciatively.

"Red is a beautiful color on you," he said. "You did very well. I'm proud of you." His hand reached to my mouth. "I'll take those panties back now."

I spit them out, my mouth feeling dry and my jaw aching. I heard Adrian toss them away to some corner of the room, and I arched my bottom up hopefully, anticipating finally getting the release I so desperately desired. Adrian noticed my tauntingly swaying hips and chuckled.

"Oh? Do you think I'm going to take you now? Do you think you've earned that already?"

Earned it? I stopped moving.

"Well? Do you?"

No. I didn't. But I wasn't going to tell *him* that. "Pleeease, Adrian," I whined. "I want you."

"Oh I can tell. But you're going to learn to be patient, little girl." He gave my thigh a little swat, gentler than before but still enough to make me jump. "Get up on the bed. Get on your knees, but keep your head down on the bed."

I did as he said, moving into position. His every command was making tingles spread out from between my legs, washing over me in waves of increasing desire. I wanted to beg him. Beg him to please, *please*give me release. But I had a feeling that would only result in him drawing this out longer.

Up on my knees I was perfectly exposed. For a few moments he didn't touch me at all, but I could feel his eyes on me. Watching my subtle, desperate squirming. Then he moved away from me, towards the end of the bed where there sat a large leather-bound chest. I turned my head to watch him, drinking in his form. He had taken off his shirt at some point, I wasn't quite sure when. His skin gleamed in the city lights.

"What is that? Sir?" I added quickly. I really didn't want any more swats. He was rummaging through the chest, and when he looked up again he looked like a wolf staring down his next meal.

"It's my toy chest," he said. "With all kinds of toys for very naughty girls. And I intend to play with you all night."

I watched from my exposed position as Adrian brought out some of his toys. He laid them side by side on the bed, watching my face as I absorbed what they would be used for. The first was a slim white wand with two buttons on the side, which I recognized immediately as a vibrator. The second was a pair of padded cuffs connected by a short chain. I stared at them, wide-eyed. Adrian picked up the cuffs, and moved behind me again.

"I'm going to show you just how desperate you can truly be for release," he said. He tapped my wrists, and I brought them immediately back behind my thighs. He cuffed them, and I was once again bound into my position. Unable to touch myself or him. I squirmed, whimpering. Why was I doing this to myself? Allowing myself to become needier and needier, the ache within me growing with every expert touch of his fingers. I knew that soon I would be absolute jelly in his hands, a quivering mess with nothing else in my brain but desire.

I couldn't wait.

"Have you used a vibrator before?" he said, once my hands were bound. He picked up the toy, clicking both the buttons to test that it was working. It buzzed to life, then its sound increased when the second button was pressed. He smiled at me from behind the buzzing tool, and I gulped nervously. I could only imagine what that would feel like pressed against my most intimate parts.

"I haven't," I said. His eyebrows shot up expectantly, and I caught myself. "I haven't, sir."

"Mmm, well then," he moved out of my sight again, back behind me. His fingers caressed my thighs, making me shiver. "This is going to be fun."

I heard the vibrator buzz to life and irrationally began to struggle, pulling at my cuffs and wriggling. Adrian's hand pressed firmly against my lower back. "Keep your back arched, Cassandra," he said. "I want to see that pretty, needy little pussy of yours."

I moaned into the bed sheet as I did as he commanded. He rubbed me first with his hand, a slow teasing motion that made me press my mouth against the coverlet. Then his hand left me, and the vibrator took his its place. I jerked at the stimulation, yelping as the powerful vibrations carried through my every nerve. My arms strained against the cuffs as my legs began to shake. It was too much. I was going to orgasm already.

"Oh god . . . Adrian . . ." I moaned, breathing in sharply as my release seemed imminent. Then suddenly, it wasn't. He had removed the vibrator.

"Nooo," I whined sharply. "No, no, Adrian please give me more!"

A swift spank made me yelp. I was unbearably frustrated, and made that obvious in the growl that quickly followed my cry. Adrian laughed, and I heard the vibrator click off.

"What was *that* sound, miss?" he said. "Did you just *snarl* at me?"

"I want *more*," I demanded, completely irrational in my desire. "I need it Adrian- Sir. Please."

"Naughty, demanding girls don't get release," he said calmly. "I think I'll just keep taking my time with you." He gave me another spank, so that I kicked my feet and whimpered in protest. "I'll keep you on the edge until you're truly crying for release."

The vibrator came to life, pressing into me again. I cried out at the pleasure, squirming and shuddering as it began to rocket me towards orgasm again. Just before I tipped over the edge, he pulled it away again. I wailed in frustration, bucking my hips and growling, "Adrian! Please!"

"You keep growling, little girl," Adrian said, disapproval in his voice. "That's very rude. Growl at me again and I'm bringing out the ruler to spank you with."

Spanked with a ruler by my professor. I would revisit that deliciously frightening scenario later. I bit my lip, struggling to control myself as he continued to torment me with the vibrator's touch. He denied me again, and again. His only commands were to remind me to arch my back, which was becoming increasingly difficult to maintain. My sex was unbearably swollen and sensitive to the slightest touches of the toy. My legs were shaking uncontrollably, and my moans had become animalistic cries, drawn out of me by every torturous touch. His last denial left me gasping, crying, my legs kicking as I babbled desperate pleas.

"Please sir, please sir, *pleeease*."

"Do you want to come, Cassandra?" His voice was heavy, rough with lust.

"*Yes*, please sir!"

I heard the vibrator click to its higher setting, so when it pressed against me again I screamed, pressing my mouth into the bed and biting down in ecstasy. Then his fingers joined the toy, filling me tightly and thrusting, drawing sounds out of me that I hadn't known I was capable of making. He gave me my release at last as I screamed his name into the blankets, my body shaking and jumping until relief came.

I was barely aware as the vibrator switched off. I felt drunk, dizzy, absolutely intoxicated with pleasure and sensation. I heard a shuffle, and moved my head a bit to get a glance back at Adrian. He had pulled off his jeans and tossed aside his Calvin Klein briefs. Oh god, he looked so good. I wiggled my hips hopefully, and this time he didn't resist me.

"God you look beautiful," he breathed. He uncuffed my hands at last, so I was free to scoot forward on the bed as he climbed behind me. His hand tangled up in my hair, pulling my face gently to the side as he pressed against me, then suddenly stopped.

"Shit," he said, sounding genuinely upset.

"What is it?" I asked softly.

"Condoms. I bought a pack earlier but I . . . they're still in my car."

I thought about it for a moment. Although my release had been achieved, I still ached for him. I wanted him inside me.

"I'm on birth control," I said. I had never stopped taking the pill after Ethan and I broke up. It had become such a habit that I really hadn't even thought about it.

Adrian rubbed at the base of my skull through my hair, a heavenly feeling. "Are you sure? I'm clean, but are you sure you're comfortable with this?"

I smiled, my eyes closed in bliss. I had never been more comfortable in life. "Yes, sir. I'm sure."

I knew he was smiling despite my eyes being closed. "I can't wait to take you, Cass." He trailed kisses down my back, still asserting his dominance with his firm hand on my head. I shivered under his affection, smiling at every gentle brush of his lips. His hands squeezed my tender cheeks, holding me as he began to press into me slowly. He moaned, so low and with such pleasure that it made my breathing quicken again. He felt exquisite inside me.

Hunching low over my back, he grasped one hand around my throat as he thrust into me. His rough breathing in my ear sent tingles down my spine. A gasp escaped him, and he said suddenly, tightly, "I want to come inside you, Cass."

Oh fuck yes. I pressed back against him eagerly and he groaned at my enthusiasm, his entire body tensing as he found release within me. Hot, sweaty, and heavy, he collapsed atop me and then rolled aside so I could breathe.

After several moments of our own tired panting, he glanced over at me and I at him.

"Wow," was all I could manage besides a tiny giggle. He smiled widely, reaching over to play with my mussed hair and softly kiss my forehead.

"This," he said, grinning mischievously, "Is going to be a fun secret to keep."

CHAPTER SEVEN

Maya knew something was up. She knew it in the way that all naturally nosey people know it: they just have some kind of supernatural sense for juicy gossip. She had been texting me in an effort to meet up for days, and I finally gave in Sunday evening. We met at the Leaf and Bean, a small coffee shop downtown in between a florist and a book shop. It was one of those places that played acoustic indie music and always had at least one or two beanie-wearing bespectacled individuals sitting in a cushy chair with their Mac laptop.

Maya tried to be sly, asking coy "how-are-you-holding-up?" questions as we ordered our lattes. But I could tell by her tight smile that she was nearly exploding with curiosity. It gave me such a thrill to know I had this secret, especially when I sat down and my bottom burned softly at the contact with a hard surface. I tried to hide the irresistible urge to bite my lip behind my coffee cup as I thought of Adrian's firm hands, his commands, the perfect control with which he brought my body to complete submission.

He had been right, too. With the rush of hormones flooding through my veins after our tryst, sharing another hour laying at ease in bed with him, I *had* felt strong. I had felt sexy and powerful.

"So where have you *been*, Casszy?" Maya said suddenly, snapping me out of my daydreams. She had been saying something about a hot guy in one of her classes, or at least I thought she had. Now her smile was frozen on her face, halfway between concern and fascination. I feigned confusion.

"What do you mean?" I said innocently, sipping my coffee.

"You've just been so hard to get ahold of lately," she said, shrugging as if it didn't really matter. "Ever since we out to Bailey's I haven't really seen you." Her eyes suddenly widened, and she looked at me in horror. "Oh my god. *Oh my god.* You're not back with Ethan are you?"

"Oh god, no, *no*, Maya," I said, probably looking like I had swallowed a lemon. "It's nothing like that. I'm just busy with classes is all."

With her fear calmed, she narrowed her eyes at me suspiciously. "Oh really? At midnight on a Saturday?"

I blinked dumbly. "What?"

"Oh god, Cass, I'm sorry, this is gonna make me sound like a creep!" Maya scrunched up her face and said softly, as if ashamed. "After I texted you asking if you wanted dinner last night, I decided that I'd just go drop it off at your house since you didn't answer. It was only because I still have your key anyway and I know you haven't really been eating or cooking or doing . . . anything really." She was leaning so far forward she was out of her seat, her eyes wide and her whisper almost a hiss in her excitement. "I wanted to wait a little bit for you to get home so I stayed and played with Charlie. And you *still* weren't home at midnight, Cass!"

I laughed nervously. My dear friend was slightly crazy, I would admit it. But at least it was a caring kind of crazy. "You waited at my house until *midnight*?"

"Well I fell asleep," she said with a little pout. "But Cass, you can't try to tell me that you were "studying" or that you went out by yourself, *without* me. Who is it Cass? *Please* tell me, it's driving me crazy! You know I won't judge you, you can get with whoever you want! Is he older? Younger? Married? Or- oh my god, is it a woman? Did Ethan make you go lesbian? Not that I'd blame you." She shrugged. "Whatever you want to do, girl." Finished, she sighed, slightly red in the face from her outburst, and waited patiently for my response.

"I don't think you can just "go lesbian," Maya," I said. "But that's not it." I pressed my lips together, carefully considering just how much I could say. "Okay . . . it is a guy-"

Maya squealed. "Oh my god I *knew* it! Who is it? Do I know him?"

The thought fluttered into my head that Adrian would probably consider it naughty to be telling someone about us. That made me think of the spanking he would probably give me for something like this. I squirmed and let out a quick sigh. Maya's eyes widened.

"Are you . . ." a slow smile spread over her face. "Are you *in love* Cassandra?"

"No!" I said quickly. For some reason the question made me feel anxious. It wasn't about love. It was just about sex. Mutual pleasure. Fun. That was all I wanted from Adrian.

Right?

"You've met him before, but you might not remember," I snickered. "The guy from the bar, Adrian. We just really hit it off and have been . . . spending time together." I shrugged, just to show how cool and detached I really was.

"Ooo, yeah, I could totally tell he was your type," Maya said. "He has that weird, sexy librarian thing going on."

Oh girl, you have no idea.

"Well that's sweet, Cass, I'm proud of you," she smiled, extremely pleased with herself for finally getting the information she wanted. "Already getting back out there. You should bring him out with us sometime-"

"It's not really that serious," I said, stuttering in my rush to convince her that it really, seriously, wasn't that serious. "We're not dating really, it's more of a friends with benefits thing."

Maya paused, giving me a little frown. "Oh. Okay. That's different for you." She tried to mask her confusion with another smile. "I always took you for the long-haul commitment type. But I mean, taking a break from relationships after a break-up is good for you! And you still have to get dick somehow right?" I laughed along with her, and though I had managed to convince her, I felt a hell of a lot less convinced myself.

CHAPTER EIGHT

I hadn't realized just how difficult it would be to try to concentrate on actually learning in Adrian's class. I had hoped that after being so satisfied our last night together, it would tame some of the raging hormones that he seemed to illicit just by being near me. I could not have been more wrong. Waiting for him to walk into class was torturous. I felt almost like I was back on his bed, tied up and waiting for him to touch me. Feeling like that, of course, led to even more problems.

"Good morning, class. Hope you all had a good weekend. Let's jump right in with Robert Frost, hopefully you all had a chance to do the reading over the weekend. If not, you may have a bit of trouble this morning." Adrian sat his briefcase down on the desk and regarded the class with that sly, cruel smile all professors seemed to get before they did something they knew would make their students groan. "Get out a piece of paper, phones away for a few minutes." There came the expected moaning and shuffling of paper. I slowly took out my notebook and pencil. Robert Frost had been the one reading I *hadn't* gotten to the previous week.

"Make sure you write down the usual, your name and the date," Kahaln began to pace, as if he was thinking over what he was about to ask only now. His eyes flickered over mine and I gave him a small, hopeful smile. It didn't seem he was going to have any pity. Strolling to the whiteboard, he picked up a marker and wrote across the board. "In no more than a paragraph, answer this question: What is the "sound of sense?" I'll give you ten minutes for this little exercise, plenty of time. Start now."

I stared at the paper in front of me blankly. What kind of English major was I that I had never read Frost? I tapped my pencil nervously and glanced up, only to see Adrian looking at me from over his glasses. He was seated at his desk, holding our textbook open on his lap, the lap I was certainly going to be over for not knowing this. He raised his eyebrows, and I mouthed silently, "Sorry."

I couldn't be absolutely certain, but it looked like he mouthed back the words "bad girl" at me. I cringed in my seat. Running out of time, I scribbled quickly on my paper,

The sound of sense is the sound of me declining to go over your knee next time.

I folded the paper before slipping it into the pile that was passed down around the room. I really did try to pay attention for the rest of the class, but Adrian kept doing little things with his mouth and hands that set me off on long daydreams about things that were not at all appropriate for a classroom. When class was finally over, I made to bolt for the door before he could discover my shameful answer.

"Miss Cassandra!" I stopped halfway up the stairs. Adrian was currently occupied with a small group of students, but he had paused in the middle of their discussion to call me. "If you would wait for just a few minutes I would like to discuss something with you."

I considered completely defying him and leaving anyway. I lingered on the steps, not coming down but not going any further up either. My face was burning at the thought of my stupid answer tucked in their amongst the others. What kind of student did that make me look like? Sure I was sleeping with him, but he was still my professor too. My grades depended on him.

When the other students cleared out, Adrian sat back down at his desk and looked up at me, dawdling sheepishly on the stairs. He crooked his finger. "Come here, Cassandra."

I really took my time getting down to him. "Yes, professor?" I was still a good six feet away from his desk. Plenty of space to run.

"Shall I grade your essay question now?" he said, already rifling through the stack of papers. "You seemed to be having a bit of trouble with it."

"No," I said quickly. "You should actually really wait. Until I'm gone. Far away. In another class."

He chuckled. "Do you think that will save your ass from me?"

Nope. Probably not. I smiled nervously, watching as he pulled out my folded piece of paper and laid it flat on the desk. It seemed like he stared at it a long time before he looked up at me. When he did, he was struggling to keep a serious face.

"Miss Cassandra," he said, mouth twitching. "I think you know this is not an acceptable answer."

My bottom twitched in anticipation. It still stung from Saturday, dammit! "I know, sir."

"Did you not have a chance to do the reading? I thought Robert Frost would be someone you would enjoy. That's why I chose him for this week. It had originally been Herman Melville."

"Oh. You did?" I was taken by surprise.

"Yes. *Acquainted with the Night* is particularly beautiful, one of my favorites." For a brief moment, he looked sincerely disappointed.

"I . . . crap . . . I'm sorry," I stuttered. "I really just . . . I forgot. I completely forgot, Adrian. Sir."

"I don't want your grades to suffer, Cass," he said, folding the paper back up and replacing it in the pile. "You're a smart girl.

This is an important class for you. I can't have you just not participating."

I hung my head, at a loss. He was right, of course. Passing this class would put me in a position to study abroad next year. "I'll read it," I said. "I promise. First thing tonight."

"Or," he said, leaning forward in his seat. "If you're free tomorrow evening, meet me in the library. I'll help you study."

"Oh! Really?"

He chuckled at my enthusiasm. "Of course. I'm still your teacher, Cass. It's my job to help you."

"Thank you, professor," I swooped in for a peck on the lips before he could stop me, and then swiftly dodged out of range and up the stairs. He couldn't exactly spank me in a library, now could he?

CHAPTER NINE

Tuesday night found me making my way across campus at a much later time than I was used to. The library was open until 11, luckily, and the sun had already gone down by the time I made my way through its high, ornate doors. The library was the oldest building on our campus; it had been there before the school itself. It had always struck me as the type of place that would attract witches, or where mysterious cults would meet in chambers hidden behind bookcases.

Adrian was waiting for me on the 4th floor. There were dozens of reading rooms on the 1st floor, but Adrian had chosen a secluded table for us near the Poetry section, or so he had told me. I couldn't see him at first when I exited the elevator. But after wandering past several shelves I spotted him at the far end, seated near the wall at a dark wood table. He had several books stacked on the round table, and already had one open before him. I paused for a few moments before alerting him to my arrival, admiring the way he rested his chin upon his open palm, his face strangely innocent, utterly absorbed in his reading. The light from the old, yellowy bulbs gave the place a warm, romantic feel, and I was glad he had chosen this spot over one of the newer, fluorescent-lit reading rooms.

Romantic . . . what the hell is wrong with me? For some reason, seeing him here was putting me dangerously close to something akin to feelings: a giddy, childlike excitement that made my mouth go dry as I looked at him. *It's not supposed to be like that, Cass. You're not ready for that. Don't get feelings involved here.*

I sighed, shook my head, and started towards him. He heard me coming and glanced up, giving me a little wave.

"Well, well. I was worried you wouldn't find me back here," he said. I pulled out the chair opposite him, setting down my bag beside my chair and pulling out my textbook.

"You're kind of hidden," I said. "It's nice up here though. Quiet."

He smiled. "I enjoy the solitude. Not many people are interested in 15th to 16th century poets, even at a school this devoted to the English language." He glanced at the rows of old volumes surrounding us. "I like the smell of the older books too."

I nodded in agreement. "That smell of dust. History. Old, worn paper touched by dozens of hands across centuries." He looked at me in surprise, an unusual expression in his eyes. It wasn't the lust I was used to seeing from him, but it was something similar. Something that gave me goose bumps nonetheless.

"Exactly," he said. "Makes me feel like a part of something . . ." He cleared his throat, breaking the spell.

"Shall we go back to Frost?" he said, tapping the page in front of him. I could see the page number he was turned to, and I quickly flipped through my textbook. It was Robert Frost's, *Acquainted with the Night*.

"I have been one acquainted with the night," Adrian began to read, softly, but his voice carrying a melodic quality that made me stare in amazement. "I have walked out in rain—and back in rain. I have outwalked the furthest city light." He glanced up at me over his glasses, a crooked smile on his face.

"You're staring," he said, amusement in his voice. "Aren't professors supposed to read to their students?" I just nodded, afraid he would stop. Luckily he looked back down at the page and went on.

"I have looked down the saddest city lane. I have passed by the watchman on his beat. And dropped my eyes, unwilling to explain."

"It's so lonely," I said, making him pause.

"It is. I think most writers are a little lonely."

"It's been quite a while since I wrote anything," I replied. I had used to jot down poetry every night, thinking of verses in the simplest things like the shadow a tree cast or a girl in a flower dress. But after a while that had faded. I hadn't found poetry in things anymore. I'd found disappoint in the mirror, jealousy in beauty. And yes, loneliness.

"You should start again," he said. "Writing has been better therapy than my money has ever bought."

I laughed, disbelieving. "*You've* been to therapy?"

"I hide my problems well." He pushed his glasses back up his nose, so that they caught the light and hid his eyes for a split-second. "Like I said, most writers are lonely. Loneliness can be comforting, or it can be sad. Sometimes very, very sad. I had to learn to make it comforting, instead."

It made my heart hurt to think of him that way. He seemed so confidant, so sure of himself. How could a man like this have any shortage of friends, or companionship? Then again, loneliness didn't have to come just from being alone. After all, I had felt my loneliness the worst *before* Ethan had left me.

"I understand that," I said. "At least you got help for what you felt. It's a lot better than what I've done so far."

He leaned forward in his chair, regarding me curiously. "And what have you done so far?"

"Ignore my problems. Pretend I don't see really obvious red flags. Drown sadness in wine and boxed macaroni and cheese."

He laughed. "That sounds . . . extremely dramatic. And unhealthy."

I shrugged, giving him a sassy little smile. "What you see is what you get. That's what you get for going home with a really drunk girl at a frat bar."

"As your professor," he said, mockingly serious. "I don't feel qualified to give you advice on your mental health." He paused, and then added. "As your friend, however, I will give you unsolicited advice as often as I feel is needed, and insist that you follow it. So we'll come back to this topic again."

My friend. The simple comment made me feel stupidly warm and fuzzy inside. But it also made me feel anxious. Anxious because it didn't quite feel like enough.

We mulled over Frost for nearly an hour, flipping back and forth between his poems for comparisons. Adrian finally told me what "sound of sense" was, and it had nothing to do with him spanking me. As the night wore on the library emptied more and more. There was no one left at all on the 4th floor with us. I rubbed my eyes, beginning to grow weary from the hours staring at tiny print.

"Getting bored of studying?" he asked, watching as I stretched back in my chair, arching my back. I nodded, flopping my head down against my hand.

He scooted his chair back slightly from the table, but didn't get up. Instead he said, "I have one more poem I would like to go over with you. Come, sit on my lap. I think I can help you get just a little bit more study time squeezed in."

I glanced around nervously, even knowing that the floor was empty besides the two of us.

"In the library?" I whispered. His expression clearly showed his displeasure at my hesitation.

"Yes, in the library," he said. "Whenever and wherever I want you is where I'll have you. But only if you earn it, remember?" He gave me a cat's grin and patted his lap. "Come. Sit."

I got up and went to him. Before I could sit properly, he had snatched me by the waist and settled me down tightly against him. I could feel his bulge through his slacks and my eyes widened, immediately turned on. He took my wrists gently in his hands and placed them on the table on either side of the book, breathing a light kiss against my neck.

"Alright, Miss Cassandra," Adrian spoke just into my ear, sending very distinct chills down my spine that settled in my lower back. "Turn to page 394."

He released my wrists, and I began to flip through the book obediently. The section I had flipped to was 19th Century Poets, and I found the verses of Anne Reeve Aldrich – whom I had never heard of – upon the page he had told me.

"This isn't part of the reading," he murmured, his lips finding those sensitive spots along my neck and taking full advantage. "But I still think it's a valuable study." His fingers dug into my hips as he ran kisses up my neck so that he could nibble at my earring. I had the irrational urge to squirm away, the stimulation hitting that odd spot again that sent waves of tension down my back.

I was smiling with excitement, unable even to concentrate on the words before me. His grip tightened again, dangerously, and he growled, "Start reading, little girl."

I cleared my throat quietly, knowing that I would really have to watch my noise this time. "Servitude," I read. "By Anne Reeve Aldrich."

Adrian's hands slipped under my shirt. They slid up my stomach and played over the surface of my bra, teasing upon the exposed parts of my breasts. I steadied my breathing, determined to resist him.

"The church was dim at vespers," I read. "My eyes were on the Rood." His fingers found their way beneath my bra. They flicked over my nipples, almost making me stutter. My breath hitched and he took a nipple between two fingers and squeezed. I closed my eyes and held my breath.

"Something wrong?" he taunted. His hands left my breasts but were now heading down. They stroked over every curve, taking in my shape as they found the top of my jeans. "Are you distracted?"

"No, sir," I said, opening my eyes determinedly. I looked back at the poem, my eyes barely focusing on the page. "But yet I felt thee near me, in every drop of blood. In-"

He had popped open the button on my jeans. He slid down the zipper, his fingers tantalizingly brushing over my panties. Not enough to truly stimulate me, but more than enough to encourage my excitement. I tried again to finish the verse, "In helpless- ah!"

His fingers had slipped beneath my panties, finding their playground on the most sensitive part of my body. It took all my focus to keep from moaning as Adrian worked circular motions over my clit, sending shudders through me. I tried to stop my legs from beginning their telltale shaking.

"Go on," he ordered. "I didn't tell you to stop reading."

"I-"

His fingers entered me. I flinched, pressing back against him, a gasp forced from my mouth at the sudden intrusion. He held me tighter, keeping me firmly on his lap as he began to slowly pump two fingers in and out. I moaned from behind my tightly pressed lips, unable to keep it back. I felt Adrian chuckle, and his fingers paused deep within me, caressing my very core.

"Keep reading, Cass," his said, his voice heavy with promise. "Don't make me punish you in here."

My backside tensed at the suggestion. I didn't even want to imagine how difficult it would be to stay quiet through one of Adrian's punishments. Or worse, what methods he would use to make *sure* I stayed quiet. I clenched my hands on the tabletop, refocusing on the words.

"In helpless, trembling bondage," I said, "My soul's weight lies on thee." His merciless fingers were going to drive me over the edge. My voice was shaking. "O call me not at dead of night, lest I should come to thee!" I moaned again as I finished the reading, bowing my head toward the table as my pleasure began to peak.

"Don't come yet," he hissed sharply, but his fingers didn't still. "We're not done yet. Your lesson isn't over."

"Aahh, please!" I moaned. I tried to tense my muscles to prevent my orgasm, but that only drove me closer. I tried to relax instead, resulting in my entire body trembling as I struggled. "I can't, Adrian," I whimpered. "I can't stop –"

His fingers immediately withdrew, and I almost cried out in frustration. With his hands on my waist he pushed me up and bent me over the table, pulling my jeans and panties down in one fluid motion. He remained seated behind me, and I heard him put his fingers in his own mouth, sucking off the taste of me.

God. Damn.

"If you can't control yourself, Miss Cassandra," he said, his voice sounding stern. "Then I'm going to have to make this a bit more unpleasant for you. Put your hands behind your back."

I obeyed, whining as I did, forcing me to lean upon the table. I wondered if I could use the safety word to stop the teasing but still get an orgasm out of it. Somehow I doubted it. One utterance of that word and everything would shut down. I ground my forehead against the book as he grasped both my wrists in his hand, holding them firmly. The fingers of his other hand then stroked over my lips and pressed against them demandingly.

"Suck," he said. "Get them nice and wet."

I took his fingers in my mouth, running my tongue over them like I desperately wanted to do to another rock-hard part of him. Satisfied, his fingers withdrew and stroked suddenly over that *other* entrance down there. I squeaked and jumped against the table, causing him to press down more firmly on my hands.

"Relax," he said. "If you're tense, it will hurt."

"I'm not sure Adrian!" I burst out, beginning to struggle against him. I'd never had anyone down there before. Even that subtle press from his fingers told me just how tight it was. He paused, luckily, and gave me a moment to breath.

"Do you want me to stop?" he said. He waited for my answer as I thought on it desperately. Of course I didn't want him to stop! I wanted him to keep going, to keep pushing, to throw me all the way to the edge and then ravage me over it. But I was scared too.

Somehow the fear made it even more delicious.

"No," I relinquished at last. "Please don't stop."

CHAPTER TEN

"Good girl," I could hear the pride in Adrian's voice as I accepted, and it made my stomach tingle. "This is for your benefit too. I need you to learn this lesson thoroughly."

His fingers, slick with my own saliva, continued to stroke over my tight opening. I tried to relax, but the motion felt wrong. How would he even manage to get one finger in there? I had to acknowledge that his touch was still sending waves of pleasure through me. Except now, every caress was punctuated by the fear that this one be the one to press inside me.

"I'm going to need you to tell me why it's so important that you pass this class, Cass," Adrian said, taking his time to ready me. "What is it you're aiming for?"

"I n-need to pass, because –" I gasped, my head shooting up from the table. His finger had entered me. It felt tight, humiliating . . . but strangely gratifying. I put my head back down with a low moan.

"Talk to me, Cass," Adrian growled, making me shudder. I wanted to obey. I wanted him to tell me I was a good girl.

"I need to pass because I want to . . . want to go abroad," I managed to get the words out before I was again consumed with sensation. He had pulled out his finger, only to immediately press it back in. How could something so small feel so tight?

"You want to go abroad," Adrian repeated. "That's right. To Europe. And how will you get there if you don't even have the discipline to get through a simple English Literature class?"

"I d-do have d-discipline." My voice was rapidly losing strength as I squirmed over the tabletop. My muscles were finally beginning to relax, as the burn caused by his finger was giving way to a peculiar, all-encompassing pleasure. I had never had something make me feel so naughty, so embarrassed, and yet so absolutely enthralled.

"Is that so?" His finger pressed deep, past his knuckle, as far as he could push it. I sobbed at the combined pain and pleasure, wishing I could grip something. Instead I could only strain against the hold Adrian had on my wrists. "If you have discipline, you would have kept up on your reading. If you had discipline, you would have been able to answer my essay question. *If you had discipline*, we wouldn't be here right now, would we Miss Cassandra?"

"No we wouldn't," I whimpered pathetically. I could feel the heat growing just below where he had entered me, my other parts begging for attention and receiving none.

"I'm going to stretch you, Cass," Adrian said suddenly, his voice leaving no room for argument. "So you remember this."

There was already no way I could possibly forget his "lesson" here. I felt the press of another finger, my whimpering now a steady stream of noise that couldn't be quieted as I wriggled and cringed in anticipation. The second finger pressed harder, making pain shoot through me.

"Stop, stop, stop," I babbled, unable to contain the fear I had of the stretching he had promised. He didn't push any further, but he did not pull out either. "I can't – no – too – too tight – Adrian please –"

"Ssshhh," he shushed. "You can say the word, Cass. I'll stop."

The word. It was right there on the tip of my tongue. Even here, in my most weakened, vulnerable state, I still had that power over him. A single word and he would stop without hesitation. That realization comforted me. He could bring me to this state of abject humiliation and yet still treat me with respect.

No more struggle, no more gasping, no pushing or stretching. But also no pleasure. No release. I would spend the rest of the evening in frustration until I could get home and give myself a meager, insufficient answer to the problem. Doubtlessly, if I was to stop him, I wouldn't be the only one going home unsatisfied. I could feel the tension in his body, the desire to have me. It gave me a bravery I hadn't known I possessed.

"You can keep going, sir," I said.

"I need you to tell me you want it." His fingers brushed tantalizingly over my cheeks, slipping beneath the small curves and appreciating every inch.

"I want it, sir," I begged. "Please. I want more."

The re-entry of his fingers – two at once – made me bite into my lip as I barely managed to hold back a primal cry of pain and pleasure. He began to slide slowly in and out, picking up speed as I opened to him. My clitoris was throbbing for attention so badly that I began to try to rub against the table beneath me.

"I expect you to pay attention in class from now on," he scolded. "Every time you don't, there will be punishment for you. I won't see you lose out on your studies on account of your desires." His left hand released my wrists suddenly, instead grasping me around my middle and pulling me back against his chest. With his arm between my breasts, he grasped my throat and he continued to punish me with his other hand. I could feel an orgasm coming, and my knees almost buckled.

"Please, sir," I cried. "Please let me cum this time."

"Don't you dare cum until I've given you permission," he hissed. All my effort was concentrated on obeying, my eyes rolling back as his fingers began to scissor as he pushed them in and out.

Are you really about to orgasm from two fingers in your ass?"

he said, low and dark against my ear. "Just wait until it's my cock inside you."

Fuck. The very idea made me weak. He was holding me up almost entirely now. I was shaking my head frantically, knowing I was going to fail. "Please, sir, I can't stop myself, please, I want to cum!"

He squeezed my throat, cutting off my air as he said, "Then cum for me, baby."

My consciousness seemed to black out for several seconds as ecstasy washed over me. I felt myself squeeze tighter around his fingers, which only heightened the overwhelming stimulation. He held me, his body hot and hard against me, and I heard him gasp as I was overcome with pleasure, "Fuck, Cass, you're so beautiful."

Next thing I knew he pulled me up and pressed me against the wall, his member out and ready. My pussy was practically begging for him. I was limp as Jello, barely able to hold myself on my own two feet. He entered me, moaning as he did, holding my wrists captive against the wall as he took his pleasure.

"Oh god, Cass," he said from between clenched teeth, pressing his face against my neck as I felt him swell within me. I clawed the wall as he released, a blissful smile spreading over my face.

Adrian walked me to my car across the lamp-lit parking lots. My legs were still shaking, and the moment we were past the last campus building, he wrapped his arm around me. My eyes widened a moment, and I almost tripped over my own feet.

"Careful," he murmured, holding me a little tighter, chuckling at me. "Do you think you'll be able to drive?"

"Yeah, I'll be fine." I almost immediately regretted answering in the affirmative. Perhaps if I said no, he would have driven me himself. I really wasn't looking forward to parting from him.

All too soon we reached my car. He didn't release me at first, instead moving me in front of him so that I was leaned back against the car. His hands explored over my body, but teasingly avoided my breasts. He stroked up my neck and held my chin, tipping my face up to him.

"I enjoy you too much, Cass," he said softly. "I really shouldn't be enjoying you at all."

I smirked at him. "Forbidden pleasures are the best right?"

He leaned down and chastely kissed my cheek. "That's the problem. It isn't just that you're forbidden." He held my eyes for a moment as he pulled away, his eyes intense with a longing I had not expected. "Drive safely. I'll see you in class tomorrow."

He left me standing there stunned. Had he really been implying that he enjoyed me as more than just a fling? But this wasn't supposed to be serious . . . there wasn't *supposed* to be feelings . . .

I got in my car, gripping the steering wheel until my knuckles turned white. That was the problem wasn't it . . . he was too good. Too appealing. As determined as I was not to fall for him – not to fall for *anyone*, let alone my own professor! – here I was, with my chest aching, wishing I could invite him back to my place. Wishing I could have him stay with me through the night.

I felt like slapping myself. I didn't even want to think that way. I was in no position to start getting feelings. I'd spent two years wasting my time loving someone. I wasn't going to make that mistake again. At least . . . not for a while.

I started my car, and flicked on my headlights. As I did, they fell upon the car parked a couple of rows over from me. It took me a moment to realize who the occupant was, his look of absolute disgust making me catch my breath.

It was Ethan, and he had seen me with Adrian.

I lagged before going into class the next day, hopping that Ethan would get there first and I could get in without attracting any attention. At the same time, I told myself I was silly for even worrying. Ethan had no claim to me, *he* had been the one to break it off. But that look of disgust on his face was unforgettable. He had been furious. I had no doubt that he had recognized Adrian. Was he psychotic enough to report it? To make Adrian lose his job and possibly his hopes of graduating?

The idea made me sick. I had to play it cool. I couldn't let him see me walk in scared.

Ethan did get into the classroom before me. When I walked in, his eyes made awkward contact with mine almost immediately. I looked away, but not quickly enough. Crap, he *knew*, he really knew. Knowing him, he wasn't going to let it go.

Once seated, I got out my notes and pretended nothing was wrong. I wrote down every bit of information on the slideshow, my hand cramping at my furious pace. Several times I glanced up to see Adrian watching me, and my stomach tightened. I could be about to cost him everything.

I couldn't stand it. I couldn't let that happen.

The moment class ended, I bolted for the door. On my way up the stairs I heard a quick, "Miss Cassandra?" from Adrian. I didn't even pause as I glanced back and said, "Sorry Mr. Blackwood, I have to get to my next class."

I felt awful for blowing him off. But if Ethan saw me lingering to talk to him again, it would only spur him on if he was already feeling tempted to report this. Could they really fire Adrian for this? After all, all Ethan had actually seen was a kiss on the cheek. Adrian was still technically a student on campus, could they hold him responsible for simply dating someone else at his own school?

Of course they can. This was the kind of crap scandals were made of.

I knew I had to tell Adrian we had been seen. But every time I opened my phone to message him, I couldn't manage to do it. What if he decided things had gotten too risky and didn't want to see me again?

That's exactly what you signed up for, stupid. I had told him from the very beginning I didn't want this to be serious. Casual, emotionless, easy sex. If one of us decided to break it off and go our own way, that wasn't supposed to be a big deal. So how the hell had it turned out that I was sitting here worrying about him protecting his own job by not seeing me anymore?

Maybe it doesn't have to be like that. We would just have to be more cautious. Only meet off campus. Not be seen with each other. That was doable.

Except we had already been seen. If Ethan wanted to do something about it, we didn't have to be caught again.

He doesn't have proof. Surely the officials aren't just going to go off the word of a jealous ex-boyfriend. If we both denied it, who were they more likely to believe?

I was still stressing when I got home that night. I flopped onto the couch, letting out a heavy sigh. I still hadn't texted Adrian, and began to think that this conversation would be more appropriate to have in a call. Charles hopped up next to me and rubbed his big fluffy body across me, as if trying to comfort me with soft fur and kitty purrs. I scratched along his back, stalling.

"What do I do Charlie?" I said. He gave a little *mrrow?* in response. "What if he won't see me anymore?"

I imagined Charles' response would be, "Then that would be for the best. If you care for something, let it go. Your individual futures are far more important than temporary pleasures. Have the respect to communicate with him what has happened, so that he may make the choice on his own."

I could interpret a lot into cat meows. My future as a crazy cat lady was confirmed.

I was out of wine, so even my liquid courage had run out. With my heart in my throat, I picked up my phone and called him. One ring. Then two. Then three. It just kept ringing. I tapped my foot impatiently.

Come on, Adrian. Now isn't the time to not answer your phone. My call went through to voicemail. Frustrated, I tossed my phone onto the couch and tried to breathe myself into relaxation.

There was nothing either of us could do about it tonight anyway. I would just have to try again tomorrow.

But that also meant worrying about it until then.

I had been staring blankly at Netflix for almost an hour when my phone buzzed. It was Adrian, apologizing for missing my call and saying he had been in a meeting. I breathed a sigh of relief to hear back from him, but now I had to actually put together the words . . .

I asked him if I could call, saying we needed to talk. He responded that he was driving, and would call me when he could. The waiting game was killing me. I began to question myself, wondering if I was making a bigger deal than I needed to.

Almost 20 minutes passed, and my phone finally rang. My hands were shaking when I picked it up.

"Hi, Adrian," I said, realizing how tense my voice sounded.

"Hi, Cass. Sorry to keep you waiting."

"It's fine. Listen, there's something we really have to talk about-"

"Wait – hold on a second –" There was a shuffling sound, like he was moving plastic bags around. "Open your door first."

I stared at my front door. *No way.* I opened it like I was antici-pating a serial killer. Adrian stood there, hanging up his phone, carrying a plastic Wal-Greens bag. He smiled that crooked, uncertain smile that gave me flutters in an entirely different way than his usual, devilish grin did.

"What . . . what are you doing here?" I asked, in disbelief.

CHAPTER ELEVEN

Adrian held up the bag he was carrying, and I could see the top of a wine bottle sticking out. "I know you were upset today," he said. "I don't know if it was me, or something else, but I've heard these things help."

I took the bag, struggling to pick my jaw up off the floor. There was a bottle of red wine – and not the cheap, bottom shelf brand I usually bought – and a half-quart of Ben & Jerry's ice cream. I picked it up, genuinely emotional at the sight of the delicious dessert.

"This is my favorite," I murmured. My eyes were actually teary. Crap. All my worry and waiting and build-up and here he was at my door with ice cream and wine.

He smiled, looking rather proud of himself. "Good. Now I know I'm unexpected. You don't have to invite me in. I can leave and we can still talk on the phone."

"No, no, for god's sake, come in, Adrian," I opened the door for him, quickly shutting it again and sticking out my leg to prevent Charles from making his escape. I was glad he was actually getting to see my apartment clean for the first time. At least this proved I wasn't a complete slob.

"Do you want some?" I said, as I searched for my wine cork in the kitchen drawers. For something I used almost every other day, I somehow managed to misplace it just as often.

"Sure," he said, leaning against the kitchen doorframe. He was wearing a tight button-up with jeans and casual black Vans. Not the kind of meeting attire I was expecting.

"What kind of meeting were you in?" I said, glancing at his shoes for emphasis as I poured us both a glass.

"It was with one of my professors," he said, accepting the glass I offered with a smile. "I actually have classes on Mondays and Wednesdays myself."

I didn't know why it had never occurred to me to ask about his own classes. Somehow it had never really solidified in my mind that a professor would still be taking classes like all the rest of the undergraduates. He followed me to the couch, where Charles promptly decided to inspect his lap and then curl up on it. I was worried he would be upset about cat hair on his clothes, put he clicked his mouth in the universal "kitty sound" and scratched under Charles chin.

"My cat likes you," I said incredulously. "And he really doesn't like anybody."

"Getting the cat the like you is on par with getting the mother to like you," Adrian said, as Charles leaned appreciatively into his hand. "Maybe even more so. You don't usually have to live with the mother."

I bit my lip, knowing what I had to tell him. I took a deep, burning gulp of the wine, and blurted out, "My ex saw us in the parking lot last night!"

Nice one, Cass. That had admittedly not been how I was intending to tell him. He looked confused at first, then he frowned. "So he saw you with another man. That's none of his business."

"He's in your class," I said, and his frown deepened. "He had to have recognized you. I saw him, and he looked so . . . angry."

Adrian swirled his wine in his glass, pinching his lower lip between his fingers. "Hmm. I see. And you think he was angry enough to tell someone? I thought he left you of his own choosing?"

"He *did*," I said, exasperated at the situation. "He's just . . . he's possessive. He's that kid that won't want a toy until someone else is playing with it."

Adrian raised an eyebrow. "Is that the kind of sociopaths you usually date?"

I blushed, feeling more than embarrassed. "I was too stupid to accept that while I was with him," I said tightly. "I didn't know . . . I mean . . . I knew. I just . . . I had spent so much time wanting it to work . . ." I shrugged uselessly.

"Don't call yourself stupid," Adrian said sternly, reaching over to tuck my hair behind my ear. "Or I'll put you over my knee." Seeing that illicit a nervous but relieved giggle out of me, Adrian turned himself on the couch to face me more fully. "Don't blame yourself. We both chose to do this, knowing it was probably really stupid. If your ex decides to go to someone at the school about it, we'll deal with that when it comes. He has no proof. It's one sociopath's word against ours."

I put my head down, staring at my curling toes. "So you . . . you would be fine with . . . still spending time with me? I mean, with still doing . . . what we've been doing?"

He looked confused as he continued to stroke my hair. "And why exactly would I let your ex scare me away from you?" he said. "A boy like that doesn't frighten me."

"School officials should," I said, still hardly able to look at him. I hated that I was so scared. I hated that I absolutely dreaded that he could walk away. I hated that I knew I would have to let him if he did. "They would fire you, Adrian. You could be kept from graduating. What if they expelled you?"

"That's for me to worry about," he said firmly. "Not you. Doing this was my choice, knowing the risks. I felt you were worth it anyway."

I wanted to ask him what exactly he'd meant when he said *I* was worth it. Surely he meant the sex was worth it, the gratification, the pleasure. That's what this was about. Still, it made me smile to hear that. I pressed my face against his hand, which had begun to toy with my ear.

"Come here," he said, and leaned back on the couch. Charles politely gave up his spot, and I laid myself down against Adrian's chest. Feeling his warmth and his arms around me made all the anxiety that had plagued me for the entire day melt away. I suddenly felt exhausted, and my eyes fluttered closed. I spent a few minutes just absorbing the closeness, relishing it. Then Adrian's fingers began to stroke gently along my arm and I practically melted.

"That feels so nice," I moaned into his chest.

"You're so tense, little girl," he said disapprovingly. "Have you been worried about this all day?"

"Yeah," I mumbled sleepily. "I couldn't focus in class. I wanted to tell you. I just . . . I thought that you . . ." I buried my face against his shirt, muffling my words. "I thought you wouldn't want to see me anymore."

He fingers paused in their caresses. I wanted to whine at him to keep going, it had felt so nice. What the hell was wrong with me? Why did this man make me weak in the best of ways?

"Is there something more you want from me, Cass?" he said slowly, as his fingers resumed their heavenly ministrations. "I know you said you wanted this to be casual. That you weren't ready so soon after your last relationship for anything requiring an emotional commitment. But I want to make sure . . . that you're alright."

I played with the buttons on his shirt. The little voice inside was beginning to frighten me. It was screaming for things I didn't want. Or at least, that I had *thought* I didn't want. I wished I could ask for a retraction of that question. But he was silent, waiting for my answer.

"I'm okay," I lied. I was glad he wasn't making me look at him. "That's still what I want."

He didn't pause, or accuse me of lying, or demand I rethink my answer. Instead he said, "Just know that I don't want to leave, Cass." He sighed, as his fingers tugged lightly at my hair. "This is happiness for me."

I tucked my head down and pressed it more tightly against him. The last thing I needed was for him to see all the emotions I had denied having suddenly welling up in my eyes.

I flinched awake the next morning, both alarmed and confused. I was held, I was warm, and Charles was asleep at my feet. A familiar scent, somewhere between fading cologne and sweet, morning sweat surrounded me. The chest I lay on was snoring softly.

Adrian had stayed the night. I was stunned. We hadn't even had sex. Wasn't spending the night supposed to be reserved for "lovey" relationships only? I didn't want to move, lest I break that peaceful moment and never be able to return. His shirt was partially unbuttoned, and at some point he had set his glasses on the coffee table, next to our empty wine glasses.

The exact opposite of what I had been afraid of was happening here. Adrian had not left. He had not dropped me at the first sign of trouble. Not only that, but I was relieved that he hadn't.

Was I actually falling for Adrian Blackwood?

Maybe the better question was, was he falling for me?

I couldn't even *let* myself consider that. But I did let myself nap a little longer snuggled up against him. Finally, I felt him beginning to stir. He sighed heavily and stretched his arms, then relaxed them around me again. I peered up at him, wide-eyed.

"Good morning."

He smiled, sleepy-eyed. "Good morning." His fingers tangled in my hair. "You have a very comfortable couch."

"You have a very comfortable chest." He grinned widely, rubbing a hand over his face as he reached for his glasses. I sat myself up, internally mourning that comfortable chest I was leaving. "Are you hungry? I can make bacon and hash browns."

"I'm starving," I watched his dark eyes adjust behind his glasses, and then he quickly checked the time on his phone. "Oh. Crap. I'm supposed to be at work in an hour." He looked down at his clothes, quickly getting up off the couch. "These will be fine. Do you mind if I shower here?"

"No problem. It's right down the hall to your right."

He was already stripping his clothes off. His bare chest aroused something in me that made me want to rake my nails across it, claiming my territory like a cat. *Except it isn't my territory. Stop thinking that way Cass.*

He paused halfway to the bathroom, glancing back at me. He was wearing white Calvin Klein's and nothing else. He tweaked one eyebrow, and said, "Join me?"

Oh hell yes. I practically leapt up off the couch, much to his amusement. The combination of morning cuddles and steadily growing hunger were swiftly getting my heat up. He stopped me just outside the bathroom and slowly began to strip my clothes off. My shirt went first, and he kissed along my stomach and up to my breasts as he peeled it off me. Then my sweatpants, which he followed down with a trail of kisses. On his knees, he gripped my hips and his finger kneaded into my cheeks.

"You know, it's very hard not to say this is mine," he said. He gave me one sharp, playful spank, making me jump. "I'm not used to failing to claim a woman entirely." He stood, reached his arms behind me, and unhooked my bra. I gazed up at him, my breathe quickening as he massaged my breasts and flicked his fingers over my nipples.

"What are your intentions with me, Mr. Blackwood?" I said, partially playfully and partially serious. So he wanted to claim me too, did he?

"My intentions," he growled. "Are to bring you to your knees with your body having been pleasured in every possible way, and when I ask you to whom you belong, for you to respond without hesitation, "yours, sir." "

I swallowed hard. *God damn, that's hot.* It was also completely contrary to our agreement of what exactly this relationship was about. But I was really beginning to care less and less about that.

"I guess you'll have to work on pleasuring me in every possible way first," I said, feeling rather daring after having seen him on his knees. That feeling almost immediately dissipated as he clasped the back of my neck in his hands, that devilish eat-you-alive smile baring down at me.

"Oh-ho, a rather demanding girl today, aren't you?" He backed me into the bathroom, breaking eye contact only to turn on the shower. "Is that really what you want? Are you sure?"

Well god damn, I wasn't too sure now! He had a way of making the simplest things sound deliciously frightening. He saw my hesitation, and his grin spread wider.

"Face the wall," he said. "And pull down your panties."

I did as he said, turning around and then kicking my panties off from around my ankles. He didn't touch me, although I longed for him to. I could feel his eyes exploring up and down my entirely naked body and I shivered. Waiting was the most difficult part. It brought out the brat in me, that wanted to whine at him to just get on with it. But I didn't dare do that. I couldn't even imagine what tortures he would inflict if I dared to demand his touch.

"Lean forward, you can rest your face on the wall," he said, as the bathroom filled with steam. "And spread your cheeks for me."

Oooh. That made a blush light up my face immediately. I leaned forward, but hesitated before fulfilling his second command. Baring myself like that, in the light of day, felt so filthily intimate. He must have become impatient with my hesitating, because his hand quickly smacked across my ass. I yelped louder than I needed to, more in protest at the spanking than in pain.

"Do as I told you," he said. "Or I'll find a plug for that little hole and force it to stay open for me."

Part of me wanted to dare him to do it. The other part was

absolutely despairing at my own masochism. Obedient at last, I grasped my cheeks in my hands and parted them. I heard him move, and out of the corner of my eyes I saw him go on his knees again.

"Keep holding yourself like that for me, Cass," he said. "Keep your back arched. Don't break your position."

I could only think that he had torture in store for me. In only a few seconds, I was proved right. His tongue began to rim me, sucking and licking where I had never expected *anyone* to willingly put their face. His hand reached up to toy with my clitoris and I began to moan, barely able to stand holding the position he had put me in. I was exposed, my skin taut beneath his tongue. My legs began to shake as I gasped with every firm lick. He paused, and I felt his face pull away a moment.

"Do you have lube?" he said. I somehow managed to shake my head. Words weren't quite a thing I was capable of at the moment. "What about Vaseline?"

"C-cabinet," I managed to get out. He got up, but I didn't dare break my position. He went to the medicine cabinet and withdrew the clear container of thick jelly.

"Get in the shower," he said, and I thankfully broke my exposed positioning to climb into the steamy stream of water. It felt fantastic, immediately warming my over-stimulated skin and soothing my muscles. He climbed in after me, setting the Vaseline on the little soap shelf.

"We're going to stretch you today, little girl," he said, his body slick and wet against mine as his hands explored me. "I'm going to claim you fully, and you're going to love every second."

***

I was terrified, but I also wanted to beg Adrian, yes, please, take me. He turned me so that my breasts were pressed against the glass shower doors, his nails clawing slowly, tantalizingly down my back. Combined with the hot water, the marks he left created a burn that made me whimper. I heard him pop the lid off of the Vaseline container, and suddenly his fingers were exploring me again, stroking around the place his tongue had so recently been.

"Hold yourself open for me," he said. "Just like you did before."

I could hardly stand it. I was so turn between humiliation and absolute pleasure. His fingers were slick, and the first one slid inside me far more easily than I remembered. I breathed slowly, carefully, relishing the slow push in and out. He would withdraw his finger completely, and then push it back in, so that every time I felt the full sensation, my muscles tensing, relaxing, and straining at the unexpected intrusion.

"Keep yourself open," he insisted. He paused with his finger within me to press in on my lower back. "Stop curling your back away from me. Arch, baby, just like that."

The enhanced position made his finger stroke even deeper, and the strain of maintaining it tightened the muscles in my abdomen in such a way that every movement felt more intense. Then a second finger entered me. This one was significantly harder to take, so I bit my lip and moaned long and low as he began to pleasure me again. I desperately wanted to touch myself, to ease the growing ache and heat between my legs. The fact that I could not was making the pleasure spread throughout my entire body, seeking stimulation in every nerve. His two fingers began to scissor, stretching my already-protesting muscles. The heat from the shower was making beads of sweat roll down my forehead, and I clenched my teeth as I turned my face to watch him.

His face was concentrated, intense. His eyes flickered between the tight entrance he was invading and my own face, watching every expression of pain and pleasure that manifested there. "How about a third finger, baby?" he murmured, and my stomach fluttered at the pet name. But I shook my head quickly.

"I want you inside me," I said. "Please Adrian. I can take it."

He smiled , and kissed my cheek. "I'm proud of you, baby. Keep yourself spread for me then."

I struggled to do as he said, as his fingers withdrew and he picked up the Vaseline again. He coated his cock with it thoroughly, and spread more over my tender entrance for good measure. Then he pressed the head against me, and I knew immediately that this was going to be entirely different from his fingers. Even from that meager pressure, the entry was protesting.

"Relax," he said soothingly. "Remember not to tense your muscles." He wrapped his arms around me and grasped my breasts in both hands as he pressed inside. I almost screamed, but instead managed to muffle it down into a series of desperate, pained gasps.

"Shhh," he whispered in my ear. "Easy, Cass. Easy. That's the worst part, already over."

Moving slowly, he pushed deeper inside me. The strangled noise that escaped my throat was somewhere me between a sob and a cry of ecstasy. I felt his lips against my neck, kissing and sucking, activating the odd sensitive spots that sent shudders down my back. As my body loosened to him his pace quickened, the fullness both strange and amazingly pleasurable.

"Please touch me," I begged. "Please. I want to cum."

He acquiesced, his fingers moving between my legs. I shuddered, and would have bent double if his other arm wasn't still holding me firmly in place. "Don't come until I give you permission," he warned. "And keep those cheeks spread. Otherwise I'll fuck you hard and won't let you cum at all."

I moaned at his demands, my hands still spreading myself open to him. The ministrations of his fingers combined with the tight, slick feeling of him sliding in and out of my ass was bringing me to orgasm far more quickly than I expected. Somehow I had to stop myself. But I was held in place, entirely helpless, unable to stop the pleasure and not allowed to give into it. His fingers pressed apart my folds so that my clitoris was taut and exposed, continuing to drive me mercilessly to my peak. My legs were weakening, my muscles squeezing unbearably tight around his length.

"Adrian, please slow down, you're going to make me cum," I sobbed, gasping in the steamy air. He mercilessly kept going, taunting my throbbing clit to my breaking point. "I can't stop, Adrian, please!"

"Obey me, Cass," he said, but I could hear the amusement in his voice. He knew I couldn't obey. He knew I was going to fail and then he could punish me for it. Sadistic fuck.

"Adrian if you let me cum, you can fuck me as hard as you want," I said, knowing I had only seconds to bargain my way out of a punishment.

"Mmm, is that so?" he very slightly slowed his rubbing, drawing out my pleasure to an impossible point. "Well. If you really want to cum that badly . . . cum for me. Now."

I gladly gave in. My cry probably carried easily through my apartment walls, disturbing every neighbor above, below, and beside me. Let them make their noise complaints. Nothing else mattered except that exquisite release.

Basking in the afterglow, but still tantalized by the feeling of him inside me, I let him move me easily. "On your hands and knees," he said, maneuvering me downwards. The water poured over me, soaking my hair. I was a mess, wet in every possible way, dazed with pleasure. "Head down. That's right, good girl. Now try not to scream."

I covered my own mouth with my hand as he pounded me. My eyes rolled back, my body torn between pleasure and pain. The stimulation was almost enough to bring me to another orgasm on its own, as Adrian expertly maneuvered my hips to allow himself the best possible angle to reach deep inside me. The water rushed around my face, dripping into my eyes, nose, and mouth. Finally, through my muffled cries he released inside me, moaning my name.

Pulling out, and pulling me up so that I sat limply against

him on the shower floor, he turned my face to kiss me passion-
ately, deeply. In between the lingering touches of his lips, he
said, "You're mine, Cass. You're mine."

CHAPTER TWELVE

I couldn't deny it anymore. I had feelings for Adrian Blackwood. The very idea of him leaving, of me never experiencing another moment together with him, made my heart hurt. But it was a different feeling than it had been with Ethan. When I worried about losing Ethan – which I often had especially during the last year we were together – it was with a desperate, frantic terror. It was with the fear of fulfilling all the ways in which he complained about me, the ultimate failure. With Adrian, I feared the loss of his conversation. The loss of the intense, fiery way he looked at me. The loss of his commands, his firm and reassuring tone. The loss of the most exquisite pleasure I had ever experienced. The loss of never knowing if he was happy or satisfied.

I absolutely *did not* want to allow myself to think, even for one second, that I was falling in love with him. But that thought was indeed there, buried at the back of my mind, prodding me more and more frequently.

"Be a good girl for me," he had said before he left, giving me one last deep kiss to remember him by. I was tingly and dazed and endorphin high even when I returned to campus for work that evening. Customers passed by in a daze. I could not remember the last day that had gone by without worry, or anxiety. The last day I had looked at my hazy reflection in windows and been so satisfied with what I saw.

Now, the only worry that lingered was this: could I bring myself to tell him I wanted more? That I couldn't linger in this casual no-man's land? Did I dare? And what would happen then? I would soon have to send in my application for the Students Abroad program, and he had promised to write my recommendation letter. What would happen when I left to Europe for a semester, possibly for a year? Did I really want to put myself in a position of having to worry if someone was waiting for me?

"Oh you've got it *bad*, girl," Maya said, shaking her head at me. I had invited her over to split the Ben & Jerry's after work, and I had yet to even say a word about Adrian.

"What do you mean?" I said, feigning as much innocence as I could. It was a pathetic attempt. She gave me slow look, her eyes fluttering as she dramatically rolled them.

"Come ooonnn, Cass," she said. "You're crushing *hard* on this "casual" guy of yours. I can see it on your face. You're all distant and dreamy." She fluttered her hands. "*And* I can smell a man all over this couch. Which means he was here for a *while*."

What kind of super-human was she? Some kind of romance sniffer dog? I gave it up, and sighed the most dramatic, overblown sigh ever sighed.

"I don't know how this happened Maya," I said. "It really was supposed to just be casual. Like a rebound from Ethan. But he's just so . . . so . . . he brought this ice cream."

She stared wide-eyed, a spoonful clamped in her mouth. "Oh honey," she said, around a mouthful of Chunky Monkey. "You've got him in the palm of your hand."

Did I? That didn't quite seem to coincide with the orders, punishments, and disciplines, and yet it somehow meshed together into a perfect system of care and trust. Maybe I was being the same naïve girl I had been for the past two years, but I genuinely couldn't imagine Adrian going out of his way to be nice just for the sake of getting what he wanted. He just . . . he wasn't like that.

He was sadistic, merciless, and absolutely perverted, but . . . he wasn't an asshole.

"Tell him how you feel," Maya said simply, like it was the easiest thing in the world. "And tell him *soon*, before everything gets too confusing, before he starts thinking about having other options."

The conundrum bothered me the entire weekend. Every easy, flirtatious text exchange with Adrian over the next several days had me itching to send a long message declaring how I felt. But I just couldn't bring myself to do it. I kept hovering uneasily between telling myself I was right to hold back, and screaming at myself for being tragically wrong, and risking losing the opportunity altogether. As Maya had said, I knew Adrian had to have other options. Just seeing the way the students looked at him told me that much.

But maybe it was meant to stay that way.

I was still stressing over my options on Friday. Adrian had been at work nearly the whole day, so I'd had plenty of time to worry without any of his usual distracting texts throughout the day. I had settled in to dinner when I heard a knock at my door. Maya never knocked, but it was late enough that Adrian could have been off work. Hoping for a surprise visit, I abandoned my dinner on the table to open the door with an anticipatory smile.

But it wasn't Adrian at all. It was Ethan.

I almost slammed the door. I should have. But forced politeness and shock took over. I stared at him, disbelieving at first and then, slowly . . . frightened. What did he want?

"Hi," he said, his voice almost mockingly cheerful. "Hope this isn't a bad time." He kept peering past me, into the apartment, as if looking for something.

"Well I was about to have dinner," I said, hating how quiet

and uncertain my voice became. "So yeah. It's kind of a bad time."

"Can I come in for a little bit?" he said, although it didn't really sound like a question. I was beginning to feel distinctly uncomfortable.

I shook my head. "No. You can't. I really don't want to see you." I was about to close the door, but his foot very firmly stopped it. I closed my eyes, taking a deep breath to steady myself. What the hell was he doing?

"Cass, I'm worried about you," he said, and I almost could have believed he was actually concerned from the wide-eyed look on his face. Almost, if I hadn't known that Ethan Carter genuinely did not feel empathy towards other humans.

"Move your fucking foot," I hissed. "I said I don't want to see you."

His hand now joined his foot, pressing against the door with an unmoveable show of strength. What was I supposed to do? Scream? Call for help? My voice felt choked up within me with my own uncertainty.

"Come on, Casszi," he said, shoving the door so that I had to step back. He let himself in, still looking around skeptically. "Don't be afraid to ask for help."

"What the *hell* are you talking about?" I began to think that this was the point at which I needed to call the police. But my phone was on the couch and Ethan had me cornered against the wall next to the door. I desperately hoped someone would walk by, *anyone*, and see what was happening.

But no one was coming. We were alone. I was alone.

Ethan's face was a mockery of concern, a carefully constructed mask over anger that I had learned to tiptoe around for years. Charles, suddenly seeing his opportunity as he wandered by, made a break for the door. I tried to stop him, but Ethan shoved me back and Charlie slipped out the door, running down the hall.

"Charles!" I called after him desperately, and Ethan slammed the door shut.

"Would you forget about that fucking cat for one minute?" He snapped. "I saw you with our *professor*, Cass. Mr. Blackwood? Yeah, I *saw* him . . ." He paused, as if searching for the words that would dig the deepest. "I saw him molesting you in the parking lot."

Molesting me? I would have laughed if I hadn't been so frightened. The very idea was so absolutely ridiculous, so ludicrously wrong, I couldn't imagine why he had chosen to phrase it that way. But as he towered over me, the cruel spark in his eye told me he *knew* he was wrong. That was the point.

"Do you think school officials won't take a rape report seriously?" he said, his voice low. He tried to touch my face and I slapped his hand away, making his anger flare. "Your perverted little professor will lose his job *immediately* Cass. As he should. He's a danger, taking advantage of female students-"

"You're full of shit!" I yelled, trying to shove him away. Instead he grabbed my arms painfully, pinning me back against the wall. Again I wanted to scream, but the sounds were stifled within me, intimidated into silence.

"Don't worry, Cass," he hissed, his breath hot on my face. I couldn't look at him. I was staring at the floor, waiting, hoping desperately he would leave. *Just leave me alone. Just leave me alone please.* "I'll make sure that perverted asshole gets what's coming to him."

"Leave him the fuck alone," I pleaded, anger and fear making me sick. I couldn't be weak. *Don't be weak Cass!* But he was stronger. I couldn't move. I couldn't fight him. I couldn't do *anything*.

"Why should I?" he laughed. "Remember, I still *care* about you, Cass. I don't want to see you get your reputation ruined."

He was relishing how scared I was. The power he had over me. "Why do you care what I do?" I said, trying not to let angry tears run down my cheeks. "Why does it fucking matter to you? *You* chose to leave me, Ethan. So why can't you just leave me alone? You don't care about me, don't pretend like you do! Just leave me and Adrian alone!"

"You and Adrian?" he mocked. This time he forced his hand on my face, stroking along my cheek in a rough, possessive way. "I just don't want you jumping into something before you're ready. I know the breakup was hard on you. I know, if you had the choice, you'd still want me back."

I tried to turn my face away, tried to shrink from his touch as much as I could. "You're crazy," I said, staring at the far wall, refusing to meet his eyes. "You're fucking crazy, Ethan."

He jerked my face towards him, his fingers pinching hard into my cheeks. I strained against it, but it was pointless. I stared up into his eyes, vibrantly blue and horrifically cruel.

"You can't just forget about me, Cass," he snarled. I knew what was coming, and I knew I couldn't avoid it. Even antici-pating it, it didn't make it an easier when his mouth crushed down on mine. The taste of his saliva was bitterly familiar. I immediately wanted to vomit. The second he let me go, I shoved him hard in the chest and stumbled away. My face was hot with tears.

"Get the fuck out," I said, jabbing my finger at the door. "Get the fuck out before I call the cops."

He left, slamming the door behind him. I rushed to it immediately, throwing the deadbolt and crumpling up into a heap on the floor, my face buried in my hands. There was an over-whelming tightness in my chest that didn't allow me to breath, let alone manage to cry beyond the silent tears streaming down my face.

I had to call someone. I had to get up. I had to find Charles. But I couldn't bring myself to open the door. I was scared to go out, scared he would still be there. Was I supposed to call the police? I stumbled over to my phone, blurry through my tear-filled eyes, and saw a text from Adrian.

Sorry I got off so late. How's your day?

I broke down in deep, hard sobs, somehow managing to press the call button. It rang twice, and then Adrian's voice came over the line.

"Hey beautiful," he said. "I've been thinking about you all day. I thought of this really-"

"Adrian," my voice cracked as I spoke. I sniffled. "Adrian, can you . . . can you please come over?"

I could sense his urgency immediately. "Of course. What's wrong?"

"I . . ." I was ashamed. Embarrassed. Why had I opened the door? Why hadn't I called for help? "I lost Charles. He got out. Please. I just . . . I need help."

"Give me ten minutes, Cass," he said. I could hear him moving things around, and the jangle of keys. "I'll be right there."

I was huddled on the couch when I heard the knock at my door. My heart immediately started pounding. Opening my phone, I called Adrian and was relieved to hear the ring on the other side of the door.

"I'm here," he said as he picked up. Sighing in relief, I unlocked the door to see him standing there, Charles already in his arms. "He was wandering by the elevators. Came right up to me."

I barely managed to gather Charlie in my arms before I started crying again. I buried my face in his thick white fur and sobbed, my shoulders shaking. I felt Adrian put his arms around me, gently leading me back into the house and shutting the door.

"Hey, hey, Cass, my god, it's okay," he said. Charles wiggled free and ran immediately to his food bowl, no worse the wear for his little adventure. My hands were shaking, the tightness in my chest making it impossible to breath. Adrian sat me back on the couch, pulled my head up and held it in his hands as I trembled and wheezed, trying to convince my body to allow me the slightest breath of air.

"Start breathing, Cass," he said gently. His fingers stroked back through my hair and massaged over my neck. With firm, careful control he pushed me back, so that I was lying against the armrest of the couch. He took my wrists in his hands and pulled them down gently to my sides. With one hand pressed against my forehead, he instructed me, "Move your legs up and open them so your hips relax. There you go. Feet together. Pull them up to release the hip muscles. Now breath please. Breath."

I did as he said. The position felt ridiculous at first, until the tension and panic began to dissipate. My lungs at last allowed me to draw a deep, trembling breath. I closed my eyes, relishing the warmth of his hand on me. The hand that was not pressed against my forehead was rubbing my arms, smooth comforting movements that coincided with my breathing.

"What did you do?" I said, still not wanting to open my eyes.

"Recline Bound Angle," he said. "It's a position in yoga. It can help ease panic and anxiety."

"It does," I muttered. "It helps." I opened my eyes, gazing at him thankfully, so quickly feeling safe again. I sat myself up, and moved over so that I could press myself against his shoulder. He responded by putting his arms around me, kissing my forehead.

"Were you that scared for Charles?" he said. "Or did something else happen?" By his tone, I knew he could already tell that it was the latter. I gave a trembling sigh, and just shook my head. I didn't want to say it. I didn't want to tell him.

"Cass," his hand stroked beneath my chin, tipping my head back to look up at him. The concern in his eyes made me want to bury myself against him even more. "What happened? Talk to me?"

"Ethan came over," I squeezed out the words, then immediately pressed myself down on his lap, burying my face there so I didn't have to look at him. I felt him tense immediately, and I felt sick. "He wouldn't leave. I told him to leave, Adrian."

"Did he hurt you?" His voice was harsh, barely controlled. I had never heard him take that tone.

"He said he would tell the school board that he had seen you molest me," I choked. "He said he would get you fired. I really did try to just make him leave-"

"I believe you, baby, but please: *did he hurt you?*" His voice was desperate, frustrated. Frightened. I pressed my face down harder, as if to muffle what I was about to say.

"He kissed me," I said, hating the way the words sounded. I wanted to curl up into the smallest possible ball. I wanted to hide. "I really did try to stop him Adrian, he just . . . I'm sorry . . ."

He rolled me over, forcing my face out of hiding, so that I lay on my back with my head in his lap. "Don't you dare apologize to me," he said, his hands shaking as they grasped my face. "Absolutely do not apologize. Did you call the cops?"

"N-no," I said slowly.

"Do you want to call them?"

I could just imagine the line of questioning. *Did you know the intruder?* Yes. My ex. *Did he physically harm you?* He forced a kiss on me. *Did he threaten violence against you?* No. There were no marks or bruises anywhere on my body. Even the red marks from the grip of his hands on my arms were quickly fading.

"No," I said softly, ashamed of my answer. I didn't want to have to tell more people, be subject to the questions and the skepticism. Besides, what good would it do?

"I understand, baby," he said. "I understand. Don't cry, baby girl. It's okay."

He held me and rubbed my back late into the night. I must have made him promise he wouldn't leave me alone half a dozen times before I finally fell asleep.

CHAPTER THIRTEEN

Adrian told me he would stay with me if I wanted to call out of work the following day. But I insisted on going. I wasn't going to let Ethan frighten me out of living my life. Not now. Not ever again. On my way in, I called my carrier to have my cell number changed. During downtime, I blocked Ethan on every social media account I had. Now I only had to worry about seeing him in public, and if he dared to come to my house again. I honestly wanted to pack up and move, but in the middle of the semester on a tight budget, it was impossible. There were only so many cheap apartment options near the university.

"You can stay with me," Adrian offered immediately. "As long as you need to."

I turned down the offer, but gladly spent the next night sleeping at his house. But the thing was that I couldn't just hide from Ethan forever. I couldn't just keep hoping he wouldn't show up. He had to be faced, in one way or another.

"Don't be scared," Adrian said, as I lay in his bed to sleep for the first time. "I won't let anything happen to you. This will be handled."

His kisses that night were fervent, his grip on me hard

enough to make my muscles ache. He tied my wrists and ankles, so that I was spread eagle beneath him. Helpless, basking in the glory of submission. His every movement - from the sharp slap of the leather crop he had pulled from within his toy chest, to the bite of his teeth along my inner thighs – left my body tingling with sensation and longing.

"Don't be afraid of the lack of control," he said, whispering down my body as he trailed the crop along my spine. "Don't be afraid to trust me."

Blindfolded and gagged, he commanded all my senses. I enjoyed the strain against my bindings, I relished struggling when I knew I couldn't escape. I trusted him. Of course I did. Every touch, every scratch, every bite, every slap, was controlled. He was conscious of my expressions, my smallest noises. He listened for the point at which my muffled shrieks reached a pitch that said the pain was too much. He pushed my limits of frustration, pushing me to the brink of orgasm only to skillfully pull me back again. Blind and bound, I could only wait for what he intended to do to me.

It was thrilling, therapeutic. It took away the worries that tormented me and made them insignificant. It forced me into the moment where there was just the two of us, just his voice commanding me and the experience of my body.

It made 3 little words that I was terrified of ever saying again press dangerously hard against my lips.

The day before class, Adrian assured me again, "Trust me. Everything will be fine."

I was torn between my trust for him and my doubts. I wanted to believe him. I just couldn't see a scenario in which everything would be "fine."

Walking to class, I saw Ethan andSophia go in ahead of me. I felt like running at her, shaking her, asking her if she knew what the person she was with was truly like. But I bit my lip. I met Ethan's gaze when it went over me. I kept my face hard and didn't let him see my intimidation. I sat in my seat at the front of the class, head up, and waited for Adrian to come. I waited for that rush of relief I always felt when I saw him.

But the professor who arrived wasn't Adrian.

"Good morning class, I'm Mrs. Tichmond. I will be taking over this class for Mr. Blackwood, who is unfortunately unable to finish out the semester due to personal circumstances."

My heart felt frozen in my chest. The woman was middle-aged, blonde hair, and wore a plethora of bug-themed brooches on her sweater that I swore I had also seen my grandmother wear. She took 10 minutes to get the projector working, but even when the lesson began I could hardly hear it. I stared blankly, my phone clutched tightly in my hands, resisting the urge to leave the classroom and call Adrian immediately.

Had Ethan already reported Adrian? But surely school officials would have talked to him . . . would have talked to *me* . . . would have done something to see if what Ethan said was even true. I thought irrationally that perhaps Adrian had been arrested, before I reminded myself that nothing we had done was *illegal*. Still my heart pounded in my chest. Fear that I had ruined things for Adrian. Ruined his opportunity to graduate, to continue working at the school. I couldn't manage to take a single note.

The moment class ended, I was already calling him. It rang, and rang again, with no answer. *Come on Adrian, what's going on?* Finally, I heard the click as he picked up. Before he could even greet me, I blurted out, "What's going on? Where were you? Why aren't you teaching?"

"Calm down Cass," he said gently, and I was relieved to hear the faint amusement in his voice. "Everything is fine. I'm in the Quad getting coffee, can you meet me there?"

"Yeah, of course." I had nearly an hour and half before my next class. There was a long walkway between the parking garage and the science labs that would take me to the Quad, so I turned and took that path. The moment I did, I heard someone call behind me.

"Cassandra!"

I glanced back, and my stomach clenched. It was Ethan.- Sophia was no longer with him. No one else was walking this way. I turned away quickly, walking faster.

"Ethan is following me, Adrian," I said softly.

"Where are you?" His voice was immediately serious.

"The walkway next to the parking garage and the science building," I tried not to sound afraid. Ethan wouldn't try anything in the middle of the day, and on the university campus. At least, I didn't think he would.

"Cass, would you stop walking and fucking talk to me?" I didn't turn around. Didn't look at him. Just kept walking, head down.

"I'll be right there, Cass," Adrian said. He sounded so calm, still in control. In the distance, I saw him round the corner to the walkway.

At the same moment, Ethan grabbed my shoulder and spun me around to face him.

"Would you stop running away from me like some freak?" Ethan was right in my face, his voice exasperated, his grip still squeezing my arms. "You ready to talk to me yet? Now that your little boyfriend has run away from class?"

"Get away from me, Ethan," I said, jerking myself out of his hands and backing away.

He scoffed. "No. I have as much right to walk here as you do. You're just-"

His voice died in his throat, and I felt another arm go around me. Protective. Possessive. Adrian had his other hand in his pocket, his eyes narrowed behind his glasses. I shrunk against him. Ethan looked him up and down skeptically, and then grinned.

"Is there a problem?" Adrian asked, and Ethan shook his head with a curled lip.

"Of course not, Mr. Blackwood," he said. "I mean, I guess now that you're not her professor anymore, it doesn't *really* matter that you're fucking my ex less than two weeks after we broke up."

"It's been three weeks, Ethan," I muttered.

"Shut up, Cass," he said, stepping forward aggressively. "Why don't you just admit that you're a nasty little ho who couldn't wait to get away from me so you could go fuck your teachers?"

I started to answer, to protest, to yell at him and ask why the hell he should even care when he didn't want to be with me anyway, but Adrian squeezed my shoulder and quieted me.

"I think you need to leave, Ethan," he said softly. "Just turn back around, and walk away."

Ethan spread his arms, pacing on the sidewalk. "It's a free country. I can walk where I want. I'm not gonna have this bitch-" he jabbed his finger at me "- and her pervy-ass professor tell me where I can't-"

Before I realized what was happening, Adrian had stepped away from me, closed the gap between him and Ethan, and punched him in the mouth. For a second both Ethan and I stared blankly, stunned, and then Ethan fell flat on his back, mouth bleeding as he stared dazedly at the sky.

Adrian turned back to me, a pained expression on his face, wiping his hand on his shirt. My mouth was hanging open.

"Probably shouldn't have done that on school property," he muttered, coming back and putting his arm around me again, leading me away as if nothing at all had happened. I was shocked into silence on the outside; on the inside, I was cheering. Adrian mused, "I really think possible suspension was worth it. How did you put up with that asshole for two years? Wait, no." He held up his hand. "Don't answer. You're going to say the reason was stupidity and then I'm going to have to spank you for calling yourself stupid."

***

I was pretty sure Ethan dropped our class altogether after that.Sophia continued to show up, alone. I tried to smile at her if I ever caught her eye. I honestly hoped that whether they were still together or not, she wouldn't have to go through the same bullshit I had.

"I left the teaching course on my own," Adrian had told me. "That's why I had that meeting with my professor. I figured since I felt like things were getting more . . . serious, despite what you said you wanted, that I should admit it to someone up front. So my professor arranged for me to do the course next year. He said it wasn't the first time this kind of thing has happened."

I was relieved, in every possible way. Ethan was no longer bothering me, and Adrian and I were no longer sneaking around campus. We met for coffee between classes, and Maya finally met him without being a drunken mess. She almost screamed when she walked by Starbucks and happened to see us sitting together.

"Oh my goooddd, you two are so *cute*," she said, giving me a suffocating hug around my chest. "Hold on, hold on, let me take a picture."

She stood back and snapped a photo of us with her phone, smiling over our cups of coffee, Adrian holding my hand across the table as I furiously blushed. It was the same photo we used later that semester to make our relationship official on Facebook.

"To whom do you belong?"

"You, sir."

Dark cotton cloth blinded me. Leather straps hugged my limbs and spread me. I was lying on my back on his bed, naked and blind. Ready and willing.

I felt the bed creak, and his breath on my face. Slim leather sensations trailed down my chest, between my breasts and over my navel. "To *whom*," he insisted, "Do you belong?"

I gulped as excited shudders flooded over me. My bindings were a promise of what was to come: I needed to be held down. Controlled. Perfectly captivated. A little smile curled my mouth, both nervous and excited. "I belong to Adrian Blackwood, sir."

The words were as sweet as sugar on my tongue. I absolutely relished saying it, and I knew how much he loved hearing it too.

Now that there was no denying it, he took every opportunity both to remind me, and to confirm with me: to whom did I belong?

The leather flogger stroked between my legs, threatening my most sensitive places with its deceivingly gentle tease. I exhaled deeply to steady the energy that was building within me, adrenaline telling me to brace for pain even as my nether regions tried to prepare for pleasure. The flogger caressed my inner thighs, making me jump and twitch as tender nerves were awoken. Down it continued to go, exploring my flesh, leaving me in wonder as to where it would strike.

"You look beautiful, Cass," Adrian's dark, gentle voice surrounded me, my guiding light in the dark. I could imagine him standing there beside the bed, blonde hair tousled, shirtless, his jeans unbuttoned, the flogger in one firm, commanding hand. The image made me bite my lip, and I almost told him he looked beautiful too.

"I love to see you like this," he said, his voice moving as he walked around the bed. I squirmed, testing my shackles just to feel the tightness with which they held me. "Helpless, needy, desperate for a touch. Entirely at my mercy."

The flogger bit across my breasts, more sting and impact than true pain. I gasped nevertheless, cut off mid breath by another solid strike. The urge to cover myself was strong, and my arms strained uselessly. Struggling in vain made me hot, even wetter than before.

"Where shall I flog you, Cass?" Adrian said curiously. "Here on your tender little nipples?" The flogger barely brushed over them. "Or on this needy pussy?" Again, the flogger taunted its potential victim. I whined at the prospect of a choice. My rational brain said to choose the former. My cruel, masochistic inner self wanted to choose the latter.

"Well?" he coaxed, when several seconds had passed without an answer from me. "Tell me what you want, baby. Or I'll choose for you."

"Pussy!" I said quickly, almost immediately regretting my choice so much that I whined some more and squirmed on the bed.

Adrian laughed. "Is that meant to be a full and complete answer, or are you insulting me? *Tell me what you want.*"

"I want you to flog my pussy, please, sir," I said, choking out the words and almost squealing as I did. The fight-or-flight was strong and I was thankful for being tied down. Although there were times now that I enjoyed struggling against him without ties, playing at denial but ever eager to give in, when he would use only the strength of his body to control me. There was a special intimacy in that, one I had come to crave just as much as the careful, methodical control he exercised with straps and chains.

"What a good girl you are," he said. "You're really trying to earn your reward today aren't you?" He paused, and in the silence I softly whimpered, wondering when the flogger would strike again. I jumped when he spoke instead. "Mmm, we are a little more limited on time then I thought. Your final starts in only an hour."

"Please don't stop!" I said. He put my studies before anything else, and had ended a session far too many times because he discovered I had not studied, or had a test coming up. There was nothing more frustrating than trying to study after being denied my release.

"I guess that just means I'll have to be harder on you baby," he said, amusement in his voice. "Hopefully a little soreness will remind you what will happen if you fail your final. You studied didn't you?"

"Yeesss," I whined, growing frustrated with the change of topic. I heard a hiss, and the flogger landed between my legs, stinging every tender bit of me. I squealed, my legs tensing as Adrian clicked his tongue in disapproval.

"Don't take that tone with me. You've really earned it now."

Adrian's floggings were merciless, shifting between slow and fast, with long pauses that made me squirm and shake with anticipation. The flogger hit my inner thighs with an unbearably growing sting, and every strike across my clit pushed me closer to being manically turned on. Before long I was gasping with every strike, my whimpers increasing in volume until he had me shrieking.

Suddenly he climbed on the bed between my legs. His breath was on my stinging thighs as I trembled and quieted my whimpering. His lips trailed kisses along my legs, his teeth occasionally nipping at my punished flesh. My gasps were now filled with breathless pleasure, desperate desire filling me. I tried to arch my back and raise myself towards him, practically demanding that he put his mouth on me.

He chuckled as he lay on his chest. His eyes were on me, taking in my readiness, my desperation: I could tell even with the blindfold on. Suddenly his finger stroked between my lower lips, slick with wetness, pressing barely within my entrance.

"You'll have to be leaving in only 10 minutes, baby girl," he said, his finger continuing to stroke over me. "I don't think that's enough time to let you cum."

"Yes it is!" I insisted, trying to strain myself closer to him. He gave me a swat with his open palm on my burning thigh, making me stop my struggling.

"Oh no, no, no, it isn't," he whispered. "Especially not for demanding girls like you. But since you look so delicious . . ."

His mouth enveloped me. I strained back, moaning as his tongue made circles around my clit, sucking and stroking. He devoured me like a starving man, and before long my volume was increasing, every muscle tense as the pleasure drove me wild. I was on the verge of orgasm, right there, so close-

His mouth left me. His breath gasped against me, hot and stimulating. I cried out for more, as demanding as ever. I knew he was smiling at me. He got up to crouch over me, kissing and sucking at my neck, his chin wet from eating me.

"Cass," he whispered, just in my ear. "To whom do you belong?"

"I belong to you, Adrian, sir," I said desperately, every bit of me aching for releasing. "Please don't stop, Adrian. Please."

"If I stop now, you'll have something to look forward to after class," he said, and I almost snarled my frustration. He grasped my chin, commanding my attention. "I may not be your professor any more, but there's still plenty I can teach you. Today's lesson is patience."

He released my wrists from their bounds, and I knew the game was over. I could not be disappointed, only frustrated and stimulated beyond belief as he slipped the blindfold off my eyes. With my hands free, I grasped his neck to pull him into a deep kiss, the kind of kiss that promised more to come – the second he would allow it. He was smiling at me, with that tight, controlled smile he wore when he was trying to maintain his stern, dominant domineer.

"Be a good girl for me," he said softly. "And come back tonight."

"You don't have to tell me twice," I said, with a cheeky smile. I was dazed as I got up from the bed to get ready for class, rushing to wash my face and brush my hair. In the mirror, I caught sight of the freshly formed marks on my neck, red and purple, broken blood vessels as a testament to our passion.

I was his. Heart and body, all his.

And he . . . he was mine.